# FAKING IT

## A Dido Hoare Mystery

# FAKING IT

A Dido Hoare Mystery

# Marianne Macdonald

This first world edition published in Great Britain 2006 by
SEVERN HOUSE PUBLISHERS LTD of
9–15 High Street, Sutton, Surrey SM1 1DF.
This first world edition published in the USA 2006 by
SEVERN HOUSE PUBLISHERS INC of
595 Madison Avenue, New York, N.Y. 10022.

British Library Cataloguing in Publication Data

Macdonald, Marianne
   Faking it. – (A Dido Hoare mystery)
   1.   Hoare, Dido (Fictitious character) - Fiction
   2.   Antiquarian booksellers - Fiction
   3.   Detective and mystery stories
   I.   Title
   823.9'14 [F]

   ISBN-13:  978-0-7278-6390-4
   ISBN-10:  0-7278-6390-8

*All Severn House titles are printed on acid-free paper.*


Typeset by Palimpsest Book Production Ltd.,
Grangemouth, Stirlingshire, Scotland.
Printed and bound in Great Britain by
MPG Books Ltd., Bodmin, Cornwall.

# Acknowledgments

R eaders often ask authors, 'Where do you get your ideas from?' The only accurate answer I have ever been able to give is that my books come from my imagination – from the way it works on everything around me. I wish I could thank everybody who has been of help to my imagination in the writing of this book. I'll try to mention a few.

First and foremost is Andrew Korn. Not only is he an excellent editor, but he has been of invaluable help in my wanderings around the internet which, as readers will understand, has proved to be essential to this story. For those who are interested in the 'howdunnit' aspect of *Faking It*, his 'Afterword' should be very illuminating; for those who are not so concerned, I will only say that if I can understand what he is saying, so can you.

Secondly, there are the others who have read earlier drafts, made suggestions, answered my questions and been encouraging: Eric Korn of ME Korn Books, Sandra Macdonald, Annie Hardy.

A special thanks goes to Ruth Guise, a reader who woke me up at the end of last November and pretty well *demanded* that I get moving on another Dido. Here you are, Ruth: I hope you like it.

Last, there is the anonymous staff writer on *The Economist*, who wrote a little page filler one week about how modern technology has changed the methods of twenty-first-century detection. It is headed by a portrait of Basil Rathbone as Sherlock Holmes, complete with pipe and frown, and the headline is: STOP OR I'LL GOOGLE YOU! I cut that out of the magazine at once and have attached it to my fridge door.

# The Runner

'*C*ASH!' It was just short of a shout. '*You gave him two thousand pounds in cash?*' Barnabas paused for long enough to get his indignation under control. Then he sighed like the long-suffering father that he is and said, 'Tell me.'

'Books' is different. I mean, buying and selling the kind of old ones that you find in a shop like mine, a shop that deals in rare books and collectable prints. If I sold tomatoes or shoes or even interesting new paperbacks, my customers would probably come and go and disappear for good without my even noticing. In fact, they probably wouldn't even come, since I run the business from an old Victorian cottage tucked two corners off the main shopping street in Islington. That's North London. But my customers come in the first place because they are on a treasure hunt, and they will come back time and again over the months and years. So do the people who sell me the books that I sell on to my customers.

My name is Dido Hoare. I am in my mid-thirties (and climbing), and my family consists of my four-year-old son Ben, my father Professor Barnabas Hoare, who taught Tudor and Elizabethan literature at Oxford until he retired about ten years ago, my older sister Pat, who bullies me when she can and fortunately is married to a doctor with a practice a little way north of London, and finally a ginger tabby cat who was named Mr Spock – because of his big ears – by my one and so far only husband, before he was murdered. You could say that I'm a bit unlucky with men. Perhaps it would be relevant to mention that I have sometimes been accused of sticking my nose into things that don't really concern me. In my own defence, I'd say that stuff happens.

1

Maybe I am more persistent than some people would like: Barnabas, for one.

It was a Tuesday morning at the beginning of February. I'd come back from walking Ben over to his nursery school and gone straight into the shop, where I locked the door behind me, switched off the security alarm, and quickly checked around. I was standing in a big room which had once been the entire ground floor of the cottage. The conversion had involved knocking out a wall or two and installing a display window and a glazed door which filled most of the front wall, and high bookshelves along the other three walls, with rows of tall bookcases back to back down the middle of the space. Today, everything out here was satisfactorily tidy. Through the open door in the back wall I could see into my office, a chaotic space in what had once been a single-storey extension containing an old-fashioned kitchen, larder and laundry room, with a door leading out into a high-walled backyard. Nowadays, the extension houses my desk, a couple of filing cabinets, folding bookshelves, cardboard boxes, and a big packing table. What concerned me at this moment was the answering machine, whose light was not flashing.

Business had been slow ever since the Christmas rush finished, and now in early February it showed no signs of picking up. I looked for something that needed to be done, but it was all a miracle of neatness, a lot neater than the horrible mess that was waiting for me upstairs. Really, I ought to go up and wash the dishes, make the beds and put away a lot of clothes. Instead I dumped some coffee grounds into the machine on top of one of the filing cabinets and switched it on. Well, maybe I ought to start choosing the books to take to the London Book Fair next weekend. Maybe business would liven up there, though somehow I doubted it. If I'd had rent or mortgage payments to make, I'd be worried, but I'm lucky that way, and I know it.

As it was, I wondered whether I wasn't just a bit bored. Maybe what I was really wanting was for something to happen? If that was it, I got my wish.

2

It had been more than three years since I'd last seen Gabriel Steen, and that was at a funeral; but I knew him the moment I saw the lanky figure swooping along on a bicycle from the direction of the cross street and dismounting with a flourish in front of my display window. I had just wandered out into the shop with a mug of black coffee in my hand and was asking myself idly whether I could get another bookcase or two in somewhere without blocking the aisles. Because old books multiply like rabbits: another fact of life. Maybe I should relieve the pressure by packing up a couple of cartons of stock to send to auction? That was the moment when I noticed what was going on outside. I watched the newcomer remove his cycling helmet and stoop to lock up his bike and went to open the door. (I keep it locked on Tuesdays, because we are only open by appointment. The idea is that I am free to catch up with postal catalogues, display problems, orders, invoices, tax records, dust, and discarded bits of bubble-wrap: all the paraphernalia of an antiquarian bookshop.)

Gabriel had aged. His lean, tanned face was more sharply lined than I remembered, and his black hair was streaked with grey. He was wearing a rucksack, which told me that he was back on business. I waved him into the office so he could show me whatever he had to offer.

Gabriel Steen was a scout – a book runner. That's someone who hunts through the stacks of second-hand reading matter in street markets, house clearances and even some charity shops for unrecognized treasures, and earns his living by selling them on to antiquarian bookshops like mine. He had turned up quite often when the business first started, but he'd vanished a few years ago without any warning. I'd thought about him sometimes, because he was a nice man, interesting. Somebody told me was living in Amsterdam.

He was looking around the room, scanning the shelves. He said, 'This is good. I see you're doing all right, Dido. Quiet morning?'

I could hear traces of his Canadian accent, though he had been on this side of the Atlantic for a couple of decades. 'Tuesdays,' I reminded him. 'We're only open by

3

appointment, and there's nobody booked in for this morning. How are you?'

He flickered a smile at me but didn't answer directly. He said, 'I have some books with me.'

'There's coffee,' I said. The machine on top of the filing cabinet gurgled a confirmation.

'Thanks,' he said. 'In a minute.'

He had found a batch of late-Victoriana somewhere, and we haggled over a numbered limited edition of *Volpone* and a first edition of *Salome*, the ones with the Beardsley illustrations. That was the serious stuff, so far as I was concerned. I passed on a first edition of Arthur Conan Doyle's *Songs of Action*. There isn't much call for his poems – or if there is, I don't know where. Gabriel also had half a dozen books of verses by totally obscure writers of the same period which I looked at only for the sake of politeness. Then a Leigh Hunt, which I put aside. Finally, we settled down at the desk with our mugs of coffee, while I got out my cheque book.

'Are you back for good?' I asked. 'I heard you were living in Holland.'

'For a while.' Something in his voice made me look more closely. He had lowered his head – he seemed to be examining the fingers of one hand, and I couldn't see his expression very clearly. 'I've been here and there. I went home for a while. Toronto. Now I'm back for a while.'

'Well,' I told him uneasily, 'call in any time. You're always welcome.' When I thought about it later, I seemed to remember something strange in his behaviour.

I watched him searching for words. In the end, he said, 'How's the baby? He must be . . .'

'Ben's four now. He's starting to read.'

A grin flickered across the weather-beaten face. 'Barnabas tutoring him?'

'You can't get away from books if you're a Hoare.' I grinned back.

But that seemed to finish the conversation. I looked for a pen. Something jangled – his mobile phone, not mine. I watched him stand up and dig jerkily into an inner pocket

4

of his waterproof black jacket. He glanced at the screen, then quickly at me.

'I've got to take this. Back in a minute.' He almost ran outside, and an uneasy curiosity made me follow him as far as the back of the shop. He had stopped by his bicycle, facing in toward the window, so I could see a succession of expressions sweep across his face. Whatever it was, something important had happened, and it was making him uneasy. But when he came back a few minutes later and found me at the desk writing out his cheque, he sat down without commenting on the phone call.

He took the cheque from me and looked at it. 'I have another book with me. Not a book really, a bound manuscript. Wait a minute.'

The rucksack was sitting on the floor by his chair. He dug down into it, past the things I'd rejected, and brought out a thick package wrapped in brown paper, which he placed gently on the front edge of my desk.

I assumed, reasonably, that he wanted me to look at the contents and reached for it, but his hand shot out and caught my wrist.

'Careful,' he said. 'It's fragile, and I think it's valuable. So please be—' He stopped abruptly.

Very carefully I picked up the little packet. It was lighter than I'd expected from its size, and wrapped tightly in several layers of paper. I unfolded them, placed the contents gingerly on top of the wrappings, looked hard, and took a sharp breath. 'What is it?'

Steen said flatly, 'I don't know.'

I discovered that I didn't even want to touch it, but I told myself not to be ridiculous, because it's my job.

The thing was a fat little volume, about six inches by eight and an inch or two thick, the leaves sewn and bound in cracking, plain yellow vellum without any writing on it. Obviously it was old. *Really* old. I lifted the front cover with one careful fingertip and found myself staring at a page of writing which I could see had been done with an old quill pen in brownish, faded ink, with decorative lines of tiny formalized flowers drawn along the top and bottom of the

5

page. The writing appeared to be in some language which I couldn't even guess at. The tops of some of the letters formed exaggerated loops to the right. Some of them looked like a 'd', or maybe an elaborate 'e'. The 'o's were pretty clear, an 's' . . . unless that was some kind of 'a'. A few of the letters appeared totally unfamiliar. Generally, the writing looked to me like a very early version of Tudor script. I turned that page gingerly and found myself staring at more of the same, with what looked like some kind of long-stemmed rose growing up the right-hand margin, this time with touches of pale, blueish green in the leaves.

'It's all like that. Some plants. A lot of astronomy, stars and planets. Some architecture. Folio sheets, sewn . . .'

I let the book fall shut. 'What is it?' I asked him again. 'Some sort of early encyclopaedia? Where did you find it?'

'Italy,' he said. 'It was in a street stall in Florence, along with a lot of rubbish. The stall-keeper said he didn't know anything about it, but his English wasn't very good, maybe I missed something. I gave him every euro I had on me, and a few dollars on top. I couldn't risk just leaving it there until I found out about it.'

'It's old. It's . . . weird! You—'

'Dido?'

I dragged my eyes away from the thing and looked across the desk at him. Something *was* wrong.

'Dido, something just came up. That phone call. I have to go. Dido, would your father know what this is?'

'Maybe,' I said. 'If he doesn't, he probably knows how to find out.' It did look like his kind of thing.

'Because I need some money,' he said. His voice was growing louder. 'It's urgent. Something's come up and I have to . . . Listen, do you want to take a share in this? If you give me two thousand pounds in cash, right away, you can keep the first thousand of whatever you sell it for, plus half of everything over. I'll put that in writing, if you like. This is out of my league, anyway, and it might take me a long time to find a buyer. And carrying it around would probably damage it. Anyway, maybe it should go to auction. What do you think?'

6

I knew that he was offering me a gamble. But how much of a gamble was it? I did the arithmetic. I looked at the volume, which had no provenance, and I really did think about saying no. But a thing like this had to be worth more than three thousand, possibly quite a bit more. Almost two hundred folios of richly illustrated manuscript, on old vellum. Date unknown. Mediaeval, surely. Old, anyway. Old is valuable. How much of a gamble could it be? I tried to picture myself watching him while he wrapped the thing up and vanished with it into the damp morning, leaving me to spend the rest of the day or of my life remembering what I'd turned down.

I was trapped.

I opened the little volume in the middle, very, very gently, and found myself staring at a circle divided into quarters, with the face of the flaming sun at the centre and four people or angels or saints, one in each quadrant, shaking an index finger at somebody – probably me.

So I composed a short document on the computer, setting out the terms of the deal as he had offered it, and including his receipt for two thousand pounds; and I printed out a copy for each of us. We each signed both of them. Then I hid my copy with the manuscript in its shabby wrappings in the middle drawer of the nearest filing cabinet.

'Dido, one more thing: can you let me have an envelope? And a stamp? I just need to . . .' His request faded into a mumble.

I dug an envelope out of the desk drawer, handed it over, and looked for a stamp while he was scribbling an address on it. There were only a few second-class stamps in the folder, which gave me a genuine business errand to do. I put a couple of them on the desk in case he needed first-class postage and watched him fold his copy of the agreement, slide it in, seal it up and use both my stamps before we set out to my bank in Upper Street. The envelope wasn't mentioned again, but I was watching him closely enough to think that he seemed a little more relaxed. We walked there in silence, side by side, Gabriel wheeling his bike. The teller in the bank counted out 47 fifty-pound notes, so that I could pay Gabriel for both the weird little manuscript and the other books . . . the very ordinary books that my – discarded – cheque had originally covered, without raising an eyebrow. I guess she was hardened to cash. I handed over the bundle of notes and watched Gabriel double it up and place it carefully in the inside pocket which also held his phone. It made a lump. That amount of cash is bulkier than you'd think.

Outside on the pavement, he turned to face me again. His eyes were blank. He said, 'Thanks, Dido. I'll be seeing you.'

Then I watched him mount his bike and ride off in the direction of the Angel. Just as he vanished behind a big, gaudy van, which was delivering groceries from one of the supermarkets, I realized that I had no way of contacting him. But it was obvious that in the circumstances he would be contacting me, wouldn't he?

# The Book

Barnabas listened to this story with his eyes fixed on my face and one hand hovering impatiently above my purchase. Part-purchase. When I finished he said, 'I don't know.'

I said, 'I know. I mean, I understand. But Barnabas, what else could I do? We've been dealing with him for years, and there's never been any problem. And look at it. This is a mediaeval illustrated manuscript!'

Barnabas said, 'I have looked. Dido, would you own such a thing as a pair of white cotton gloves?'

I just looked at him. I am as likely to own white cotton gloves as a diamond tiara.

Barnabas sighed. 'Well, maybe we could . . . Isn't there a chemist's shop in the main road?'

I blinked and nodded.

My father sighed again. 'You do know that a document of such an age should never be handled with the bare hands? They will stock latex gloves over there. That will do for the moment. Don't touch this until I get back. And don't show it to anybody who wanders in, however tempted you might be.'

I assured him that I would control my enthusiasm.

He glared. 'And find that digital camera of yours. I want to photograph every folio of this when I get back. Then I'm going to take it away. Home first, then probably the British Library.'

I said that I'd be very happy if he could find out what it was. He said that he would too, but I thought I caught a note of anxiety in his tone.

'You're all right, Dido? You won't need my presence for the rest of the day?'

'I'll just get some work done,' I said meekly. And I spent the next twenty minutes trying, but it wasn't easy to concentrate.

Afterwards, my father's plans were disrupted by the fact that it took more time than he had expected for the two of us to clear the desk, find the right position, move cautiously through the pages of the little volume, and get a sharp image of each. At first we kept being distracted by the sudden ideas which made Barnabas remove the book from the camera's gaze and stare fixedly at some curiosity. There were curiosities on nearly every page. After a while, I stopped even seeing what was there, concentrated on getting clear images and not worrying about their content. Even at that, we had worked through the lunch hour and part way into the afternoon before the job was finished and I was downloading the last images on to the computer while Barnabas remarked on his own bewilderment.

I know my father's prejudices. I said, 'I'll have to go out and buy a couple of new colour cartridges, and then I'll print out a complete set of these for you.'

Barnabas frowned. 'I agree it would be better to carry the photographs about, not the volume itself. I am a little worried about the fragility of the vellum.'

'How old is it?' I asked.

I thought the question was reasonable, but my father hesitated. 'I don't know. I assume you have noticed that there is no copyright information.' His tone was a little sarcastic. He shot me a look. 'I'm sorry,' he said. 'I don't think I've ever before been faced by something which is so obviously meaningful, and at the same time so utterly beyond me.'

'What language is it?' I asked, not for the first time that day.

'I still have no idea. The letters mostly resemble the usual Latin alphabet, in forms which I have seen in English documents dating from the thirteenth though the sixteenth centuries. Or possibly an early Italian, though the distribution patterns seem . . . Perhaps a dialect such as Friulian? Or a Baltic language might be . . . Well.'

My father can read seven or eight languages, more or less,

10

including both Latin and ancient Greek, and I understood that his failure to make any progress here was bothering him.

He said suddenly, 'Do you have a mirror? And where is the magnifying glass?'

The magnifying glass was in the top drawer of the desk. I handed it over. He passed the lens slowly over the writing on a randomly chosen page and grunted. 'All this shows is that the ink has spread slightly into the fibres of the vellum, as you would expect.'

Silently I handed over the little make-up mirror that lives in my shoulder bag and watched him hold the book up to it, focus, frown, and shake his head. 'I wondered for a moment whether it might be mirror writing. But I don't think so. Dido, what are you intending to do with this?'

'Sell it,' I suggested hopefully.

'Before that.'

'You said you wanted to research it. British Library? Your old-boys network?'

'Where,' he spoke slowly and clearly as if to a small child, 'do you intend to keep it?'

'You mean, in case it turns out to be worth millions?'

'More or less.' The very idea seemed to leave him uneasy.

I thought about it. 'I could ask Leonard Stockton to keep it for me. Lawyers have safes for valuable documents.'

Barnabas nodded and commanded, 'Ring him. Do it right now. At the same time you might care to show him the agreement you signed and ask whether it could be contested.'

I didn't even bother to ask him why. I just made the phone call, found that my solicitor was available for a few minutes at four o'clock, and agreed with Barnabas that he should accompany me there, in a taxi for safety's sake. It left enough time for us to get a sandwich and a cup of tea upstairs. I was hoping that some food would help me to see this whole business more clearly. I set the answering machine and the security alarm before we left. Barnabas was scowling and hiding the package under his arm. I saw him look carefully up and down the street while I was locking the door, which did strike me as a little overanxious.

# Nerves

Something woke me in the night for no particular reason. Perhaps my father's uneasiness was catching. Nothing was stirring. I listened to Ben's steady breathing from the other side of the room. Mr Spock was an unmoving weight at the foot of the bed. I turned my head to the illuminated dial of the alarm clock. Just coming up to 3 a.m. I wriggled down a little deeper under the duvet, closed my eyes again, and found images of strange curly handwriting and unreal flowers dancing under my eyelids. Three o'clock in the morning is my favourite time for panics and regrets. I'd be having nightmares next. I pulled a pillow over my head and settled down to wait for dawn, but I fell asleep again before it arrived.

And for the next couple of days nothing much happened, except that my assistant, Ernie Weekes, came in with some ink cartridges on the Wednesday afternoon and printed out a full set of the digital photographs. After that, Barnabas was busy with them somewhere, and although he phoned me every morning, as he always does, he had nothing to report except that he was feeling well and working on our case.

Friday lunchtime, Jeff Dylan, an old friend who runs a bookshop in Swansea, rang to talk about the book fair in Russell Square which we were both attending at the weekend. Just before he rang off he said, 'Oh, Dido, did you hear about Gabriel Steen?'

I think I guessed then, but as soon as I'd caught my breath I asked, 'What about him?'

'He's dead. It happened a couple of days ago. He was on that bike of his, and a car hit him. You used to do business with him, didn't you? Have you seen him lately?'

I opened my mouth to say, *Yes, I knew that he was back, he was in here just last Tuesday*. Something stopped the words. I discovered that I was clenching my free hand, with my fingernails digging into my palm. I asked him, 'Wasn't he living in Amsterdam or something? Is that where it happened?'

Jeff's voice said something, but I barely heard him because I was dealing with something like a wave of panic. I pulled myself together. 'I didn't know. How did you hear about it?'

'Somebody reported it in the "Books and Things Newsletter". Don't you get that?'

He was talking about a gossipy trade newsletter which arrives by e-mail every Thursday. It was probably still sitting in my inbox: I'd better look at it. So I told him that some customers had just come in and I'd have to get back to work, but I'd see him at the book fair, and then I hung up and sat staring into space for a few minutes, seeing Gabriel Steen's face hovering in the air on the other side of the desk.

# About the Man Who Wasn't
# Really News

I've just heard some bad news. Some of you will
remember Gabriel Steen, the London-based book
scout who used to turn up on his bike, a couple
of years back, usually with some pretty good
stuff. His body was found not far from here on
Tuesday night. He was riding his bike on the
eastbound carriageway of the A12 when he was
hit by a car and suffered serious head injuries.
They say he died on the spot. They're looking
for a hit-and-run driver. If I hear anything more
e.g. about his funeral etc. I'll post it here.

Ken Brown          *brownbooks@hotmail.com*

The name just about rang a bell. Ken Brown runs a postal
business from his home. I'd had his catalogues, and seen
him at the occasional book fair. I thought about it for three
minutes and then decided to be aghast. I clicked on my
e-mail and wrote:

Ken, how awful! I didn't see anything about Gabriel
Steen's accident in the news. How did you hear?
Have they caught the driver yet? Please let me
know about the funeral.
Dido Hoare

It seemed vague enough, yet sincere, so I sent it; and about
three hours later I got a colourless acknowledgement. This

14

told me that maybe I had been a little too careful. But exactly how do you find out everything about the accidental death of a man who isn't famous, who has never been even slightly newsworthy?

Part of the answer turned up early that afternoon.

Ernie Weekes has been my regular part-time assistant for the past couple of years. It's true that he looks more like a gangster than a bookseller's assistant – he's shorter than me, but broad, tough, black, always dressed in the latest bad-boy fashion – and he's my friend. He comes in on Saturdays, and any half day, especially Wednesdays and Fridays, when he has time free from his computer studies at the university up the Holloway Road. While he's here, he provides two things: enough muscle to shift any number of books, and the technological skills to design my website, fix anything that goes mysteriously wrong, and generally make my computer happy. Also, on one or two occasions in the past he has squared his shoulders, deleted his normal friendly grin, and frightened off serious trouble. When you run a shop, you can never be sure what will walk in off the street.

I fell on him. 'Ernie! Listen, I need you to do something.' I bundled him around the two browsing customers and into the office.

He looked at my dark computer screen and said, 'You crashed it again?'

I lowered my voice to a mutter. 'I just need you to find out what happened to somebody, and where, and how and . . . anything about him. Everything about it. I'll explain when we're alone, but his name was Gabriel Steen. He was here on Tuesday morning, and he was killed in a traffic accident Tuesday night. The computer's sleeping, and I've left some details on the screen. Go!'

He smiled happily, deposited his rucksack on the floor under the packing table, flung his new second-hand black leather jacket on to a hook beside the door, and bounced enthusiastically into the chair at the desk. Then I could slip back into the shop myself, and saunter with a welcoming smile toward the customer who was leafing methodically through my slightly worn ex-library copy of a nineteenth-century children's book strangely called *A Key to Mozley's Improved Walkingame's Tutor's Assistant Containing answers . . . with the full solutions*. 'Full solutions.' Yes . . .

By four thirty we'd managed to move on a bit. I'd sold some books, and Ernie had located the website of a newspaper based in Chelmsford which had only that day published a paragraph about the hit-and-run death of a cycling stranger just outside Ingatestone. It simply confirmed what I'd already found out. The internet had offered no information about Gabriel Steen that I didn't already know, though Ernie had located a human-interest article about him from the books section of the *Guardian* which had been reprinted in one of the booksellers' periodicals. It had played up his eccentricities and his nose for a good bargain, but it was only a weekend space-filler. I'd probably read it at the time, but I'd certainly forgotten what it said.

''F you don't mind paying,' Ernie offered, 'I can find out if he's got any criminal convictions.'

I was frustrated enough to agree to this daft suggestion, tossed him one of my credit cards, and ten minutes later received absolutely nothing in return for my thirty pounds. There were several good reasons why it was time to call it a day.

'I'm going to go and get Ben from nursery now,' I decided aloud. 'Can you hold the fort? If you're all right for another couple of hours, I'll take him straight upstairs when we get back. I've already put three stacks of books for the book fair on the packing table. You could put them into boxes if you have a chance. And are you all right for tomorrow? Barnabas might not be coming in.'

'Sure,' he said firmly and turned without any further comment to the shop, where a new customer had just appeared. Maybe my business was starting to improve after all.

Ben's nursery is a ten-minute brisk walk across the Essex Road and up a side street, and my journey gave me time to ask myself just what I thought I was doing? I'd told Ernie that I'd been upset by Steen's death and left it at that. Even to me, it sounded more like a thin excuse than an explanation, and if . . . no, *when* Barnabas found out what I was doing, he wouldn't accept it for one minute.

There were things about Steen's visit that made no sense. The manuscript was the biggest mystery, of course; but as I went back, step by step, through my memories of that afternoon, I focussed on the phone call he had received and his odd reaction to it. That was the point at which something had changed. In a flash. The phone call was the main reason why Steen had talked me into a reckless partnership with him – a man I had known for a long time but not very well, and who had, almost immediately, vanished forever. Leonard Stockton had told me that my home-made written agreement looked legal enough 'for most purposes', and he had locked up my copy with the manuscript. But where had Steen's copy gone, in that envelope I'd given him? And from that question, it was only a small step to wondering whether the bundle of bank notes had been on his body when it was found. When I started to ask myself that question, the idea of an attack and a robbery slid into my mind and refused to be dislodged. Naturally.

I was so busy thinking about this that I stepped out to cross a busy road without looking even one way, much less two, and it took a horn blast from a braking car to wake me up. Now, that would have been a nasty coincidence.

I walked on more carefully.

# Ask an Expert

**B**en and I were in the kitchen an hour later, just dealing with his supper-time banana yoghurt. Mr Spock was with us. He had been concentrating on scraping up another molecule of cat food from his spotless bowl, but finally he gave up, leaped on to the draining board, and began to wash behind his ears. Ben gave a jaw-cracking yawn, and I found myself imitating him. Then the buzzer on the downstairs door blipped twice in quick succession and I heard the door open and then slam shut. Barnabas had arrived. I listened to his footsteps on the stairs, and it struck me that they were dragging. He must be tired too. I went to meet him with Ben and Mr Spock at my heels, and the four of us went straight on into the sitting room.

My flat is the upper floor of the building. Its small bedroom, bigger sitting room, tiny bathroom and minute kitchen are all crammed into a space exactly the size of the shop. Most of the time it can feel cramped. I have learned by experience that a baby takes up much more space as he grows up.

Ben waited until Barnabas sank on to the settee in front of the windows, then plonked himself down beside his grandfather. I yawned rudely, fell into an armchair, and asked, 'Any luck?'

Barnabas had been unusually absent for the past couple of days, and getting a few answers now would have made me very grateful. But I realized that I wasn't going to be happy yet when he shook his head slowly and said, 'Not really, but I thought I ought to drop in on my way home. I can't say why I'm uneasy about all this, but since you told me about Steen's accident . . . well!'

'Well!' Ben echoed his grandfather's voice precisely, which meant that he was going to enter the conversation, and I thought that maybe we should put off this discussion for a while.

'Could you read him a bedtime story?' I suggested. 'And then, have you eaten? I haven't had time to cook anything. Chinese takeaway, maybe?'

'Pizza,' my father said thoughtfully, and Ben handed him a copy of *The Gruffalo*, which had been his favourite book ever since it turned up under the Christmas tree.

An hour later there was silence from the bedroom, and Barnabas and I were politely offering each other the last slice of the pizza from the takeaway in the Essex Road. I sucked a shred of caramelized onion from between my teeth and decided it was time to explain.

'Basically,' I summarized, 'Ernie has found out where Gabriel's body was discovered and what the police said about that at the time, but it's not very much.'

'Precisely what were you looking to find?'

I hesitated and found myself being examined closely. This is nothing new. I started slowly, working it out as I went along. 'I'm uneasy.'

Barnabas raised an eyebrow and demonstrated that he was still waiting.

*All right, then.*

'While he was here, something happened. I don't know if I told you this before, but he took a call on his mobile and right after that he brought out the manuscript and told me he wanted some cash. He *needed* some cash, I mean. And then when he got it he rushed off and had the accident.'

'Riding a bicycle on a trunk road during the hours of darkness,' Barnabas pointed out as I ground to a halt, 'is not sensible behaviour. Traffic is far too heavy these days, and I have a theory that many drivers are insane. Almost everybody behind the wheel of a car these days is being driven mad by the traffic.'

I waited.

He said, 'Well? What?'

19

'I don't know. All right, I did wonder whether he was still carrying the cash when he was found, and whether anybody knew that he had it. And then I wondered about the manuscript and who might have known about that.'

Barnabas reared back and snorted. 'Your imagination is running away with you tonight!'

'Maybe,' I persisted. 'But I know that *you* thought there was something about the manuscript the moment you saw it, and we have to find out about it as soon as possible. What it is. Whether it's worth thousands. Tens or hundreds of thousands.'

'Whether it's worth killing somebody for?' Barnabas said drily. 'All right, hard as it is to credit, I am prepared to consider that dramatic possibility. And I have been working very hard on the manuscript, I can assure you, though with limited results. There are signs of early scientific interests in the illustrations, as you know, and that really ought to help me date it. I know of manuscripts in collections, private and public, both here and abroad, which look *much* like this one. But the text remains a mystery. It is certainly encoded. The distribution of word lengths is quite wrong for a natural language, though right for certain ciphers. Roger Bacon, for example, is known to have written in a cipher which does perhaps resemble . . .' He frowned and cut the sentence short. 'No, no, if I let myself speculate too much at this stage, it will merely send us off on a wild goose chase. Better keep an open mind until I can compare other texts in detail. Meanwhile, I strongly suggest that you tell nobody you have it, and try to think about other things. Business? We are approaching the second weekend in the month, so there is a book fair this Sunday, unless my calculations are hopelessly astray. I shall take the day off and Ben and I will spend it together. Can you manage tomorrow without my help?'

'Ernie's coming in for the whole day,' I assured him.

I wondered whether he had really forgotten about the agreement that Steen had put into the envelope and, presumably, posted somewhere. I certainly hadn't. And that was when I admitted to myself that I could use some answers from someone who might know where to ask the right questions. As soon as Barnabas had left, I woke myself up for long enough to dig the phone out from under the papers on the little writing desk.

# Up to Something

It was after ten o'clock on Saturday morning when the unmistakable shape of Chris Kennedy's old Jaguar convertible slid past the front of the shop and stopped across the road in his favourite illegal parking space. I was standing at the door with the keys still in my hand, so I waited for him to unfold himself from the low-slung car and stride across toward me. I had the door open by the time he arrived.

'On your own today?'

'Until Ernie gets here. He phoned from the bus. He'll be here any minute. Then I have to get back upstairs to Ben.'

He leaned down and kissed me lightly on the lips, and we retired into the office, where he stared meaningfully at the contents of the coffee maker until I filled two mugs and we settled down on opposite sides of the desk. I watched him for a moment – a tall, vigorous man with spiky red hair, a nose like a hawk's beak (appropriate for poking into things and finding out the facts) and hazel eyes which seemed to be watching me in a speculative sort of way at the moment.

I broke first. 'Chris, did you get anything?'

It took him a moment to speak, time which he filled by taking a mouthful of the coffee and continuing to stare at me.

'You're up to something,' he said. 'I made a couple of phone calls, but I don't know whether I've got what you want. What *do* you want? Explain it to me. I think you might have been asleep when we were talking last night.'

The thing about Chris is that he's an investigative journalist working for one of the big London newspapers, and in his professional capacity he has contacts with a number of police departments. I've called on him for information before now. In fact, I'm deep in his debt for old favours – so deep that it would take a lot of fresh coffee to pay him off.

I told him about Gabriel Steen. Not every detail of his visit, but the outlines. I watched him listening, mentally sorting, categorizing – and finally nodding.

'Then I did get something for you. They haven't made anything public, but there's certainly a question or two about his death. They've done the autopsy, of course, and something is worrying them. Their first assumption obviously was that this was a simple hit-and-run accident, and they did put out a call to look for a damaged vehicle in the area. But of course it happened on an A road, and the car could be anywhere by now. Then somebody got around to looking at the bicycle and wondered why it wasn't showing any real signs of damage. It seemed as though he wasn't actually riding it when he was hit. But because nobody had reported seeing the accident, they assumed that it had happened after dark, and they say that he could have stopped to take a leak at the time. Or roll up. Or even look at a road map to see how much further he had to go. But as soon as they got the autopsy report they realized that the serious injuries were confined to his head – there was nothing on his body except a couple of minor abrasions.'

I told him I wasn't sure what this meant.

'They aren't sure, either, but they're wondering whether somebody attacked him and drove both the body and the bicycle out there in a car or a van. Maybe it was a robbery that went wrong? Dido, they'd like to know whether he had anything valuable on him when you saw him?'

'Over two thousand pounds in fifty-pound notes,' I mumbled. 'I don't suppose the money was still there?'

He set the mug down hard. 'You'd better tell them about that. Are you sure?'

I told him that I couldn't be sure, because there had been a gap of some hours between my giving him the cash and his body being discovered; but he took a mobile phone from his pocket, pressed a couple of buttons, and said, 'It was a DI Quinn that I spoke to. He's the Deputy Investigating

Officer on this case, stationed in Chelmsford. I said I'd contact him if I found out anything that might help his operation. He'll need the details. Anything you can give him.' He raised an enquiring eyebrow.

I took the phone from him, thought about it for a moment, and pressed the final button.

The voice in my ear said, 'Quinn.'

'Chris Kennedy said I should phone you. It's about Gabriel Steen. I'm—'

'Ms Hoare? Good.' I threw a look at Chris. I'd been discussed. I decided to ask him about that afterwards.

'He was in my shop last Tuesday morning. I run an antiquarian bookshop. He had some items that he wanted me to look at, and I bought a few of them. He asked me to pay for them in cash. What I was wondering was how much money you found on his body? You see, I took him to my bank, and when he left here, he was carrying over two thousand pounds, mostly in fifty-pound notes.'

There was a short silence which probably indicated a sort of 'Ah-ha!' before the voice said slowly, 'Thank you. No, he didn't have anything like that on him. But what time did he leave you? Is it possible he'd deposited it in a bank afterwards? I don't suppose he said anything to you? He didn't tell you where he was going, did he?'

'No, he just . . . went. He'd got a phone call while he was here and I had the impression that he was anxious to deal with whatever that was about. He was in a big hurry after that. But . . . I think it must have been about ten thirty or eleven when he left Islington. Mid-morning, anyway. I don't really remember.'

'Well,' the voice said slowly, 'I'd like to thank you and Mr Kennedy for getting in touch.' There was another pause. 'You can't tell me anything about where he was staying in this country? We believe that he was living in Amsterdam.'

I admitted that I had no idea, and I was promising to get in touch if anything came to mind, when something did.

'One other thing,' I said mostly out of a vague uneasiness. 'He asked me to give him an envelope and stamp just before he left. He put a receipt for one of the things

I'd bought from him into the envelope and addressed it –
only I didn't see the address. But you'd recognize the envelope if he had it on him, because I didn't have any first-
class stamps, so there were two second-class stamps on it.
I don't suppose it was in his pocket when he . . . he was
found?'

There was another silence, and the sound of papers being
shuffled. The answer was no.

But then he'd had hours to drop it into a postbox, which
presumably meant that our agreement was well on its way
to somewhere. He'd had time to deposit my cash in some
bank account somewhere, too. Another interruption in the
chain of facts. Probably not significant.

The silence lasted long enough for me to decide that I'd
done my duty and this conversation had run out of steam.
Quinn broke in with an invitation to take myself around to
my local police station to make a short statement for the
investigating team. The Islington station would be in touch
to arrange a time. I had to agree – at least it was a way to
maintain communications, I told myself.

Then I babbled something about being shocked, about how
Gabriel had been riding his bike around the street markets
and the antiquarian bookshops for years without any close
calls that I'd ever heard of. He had always been careful. Or
lucky. Then because I'd remembered what they had told
Chris about his injuries, I heard myself saying, 'So I was
surprised when I heard what had happened. You see, I've
never seen him on his bike without wearing his safety helmet.
When he left here, he was in a hurry, but he still stopped to
put it on. I thought that he always wore it.'

'Ms Hoare?'

'Yes?'

'Could you describe the helmet?'

I told Quinn it was just a cycling helmet, the usual stream-
lined shape, dark blue with maybe some kind of white stripe,
and hung up wondering why he had asked.

Well, naturally, because it hadn't been on the body. Because
they hadn't found it. One more little piece fell into place. It
had been, as they say, a suspicious death.

I switched off the phone, handed it back to its eaves-dropping owner, and stared at the desktop.

'No helmet?'

'I don't think they found one.'

Chris said, 'I wonder what really happened?'

I already knew what I was thinking. Gabriel Steen had been carrying a manuscript of mysterious origin and nature, and quite possibly of great value. Somebody must have known about it. And now there was the other thing. Somewhere, floating around, possibly on its way to wher-ever Gabriel Steen had been living but possibly not, was a formal-looking piece of paper which gave away the fact that Dido Hoare of George Street, London, had become involved with the manuscript and probably knew exactly where it was now.

Unless the whole thing was just bad luck and meaning-less?

I don't believe in fairy tales.

I said, 'Chris, there's something else I think I'd better tell you.' I'd barely opened my mouth when the bell of the big church just down the street began to chime eleven o'clock. Opening time, and I was still single-handed in the shop. I compromised by switching on the computer and opening the file with the digital images of the strange folios. Then I made way for Chris, said, 'This is what I got from Gabriel,' and went and unlocked the door.

It was about about two minutes before he was at my elbow asking, urgently, 'What is it?'

Our first enthusiastic customer was still somewhere on the way to us, so I had time to explain. Or try.

He frowned. 'What does Barnabas say about it?'

'That it's very, very peculiar and it'll take him a lot of work to find out what it is.'

'Valuable?'

'Well,' I admitted, 'I think so. And I'm wondering whether somebody found out about it and thought it was worth enough to kill for. But I'm trying to tell you something: you know that envelope I was asking Quinn about? The one Gabriel had when he left here? It held a kind of formal agreement that we'd signed. He sold me a half-share in the thing. Wait a minute: the agreement is still on the computer.'

I opened the document for him to read. While he was looking, I threw a few books for the fair into the nearest empty cardboard box.

'Dido?'

'Yes?'

He hesitated for long enough to show me that he was thinking about it all very carefully. Then he said, 'Oh-oh,' and he was probably right, too.

# The Visitor

E arly Monday evening, I pulled up on the yellow line in front of the shop so that Ernie and I could unload the folding shelves into the corner of the office where I store them between book fairs and stack the boxes of books by the office door to wait for their unpacking and re-shelving the next morning.

Then I paid Ernie for his weekend hours with a handful of cash from what I had taken at the fair, told him that if he really had time the following morning to pop in, I could certainly use some help, locked the shop, and staggered upstairs to the flat where I was hugged by Ben, miaowed at severely by Mr Spock, and assured by my father that all was well and a delivery of pizza would arrive shortly – from the 'decent' place in Crouch End where they actually knew how to build an authentic Italian pizza, unlike the English imitations available locally.

I was asleep before ten. Book fair days are like that. But by nine thirty on Tuesday morning, as I was strolling back from Ben's nursery school with a bag holding a carton of milk and a muesli bar, I decided that I was probably awake again. I rounded the corner and, as I waited at the kerb for a car to pass, decided that the breakfast dishes could wait, and went straight into the shop to make sure everything was all right.

The boxes were still waiting for me. Fourteen. I really only wanted to unpack the one which held my own purchases. All those books had to be checked, researched, priced and shelved. The rest could be dealt with during the day. I couldn't remember whether I had any appointments, so I opened my desk diary, found it blank, and then turned my attention to the flashing red light on the answering machine. I unwrapped one end of the muesli bar, took a bite, and pressed the button.

The first message had been waiting for me since the previous day, and the voice belonged to someone I'd met a few months back.

'Ms Hoare? This is Laura Smiley, over at the police station. I guess you'll know what this is about. We've had a fax from a DI Quinn in Chelmsford. Can you phone me as soon as possible, please?'

Um. In a minute. I went through the rest of them, made a couple of notes – business matters – and finished with a brief silent call which I put down to a wrong number. I started the coffee maker and went to get the carton of books I'd just bought and undid the flaps so I could start looking at things while it was brewing. Nice things first.

The last of the nice things was something I would be able to sell eventually, but I'd actually bought it with mixed motives. It was a mid-nineteenth-century book by somebody called H. Noel Humphreys, bound in red cloth gilt: the title was *Specimens of Illuminated Manuscripts of the Middle Ages*. I'd noticed it on Monday afternoon just as the book fair had been winding down, and I'd bought it on impulse after a minimum of bargaining and some thinking aloud that I'd like to give it to Barnabas for his birthday. I probably wouldn't even lose money on the deal. The book included twelve mounted colour plates of manuscripts, several of which had struck me as both like and unlike the thing resting in my lawyer's safe.

I was still looking at them when I heard the shop door rattle. The rattle was followed by a ring of the bell. I peered through the open office door. The man who was standing there was a stranger. He raised his hand and rang again, a longer ring. I got to my feet, strolled out, and confirmed my first impressions. A middle-aged man was staring back at me through the glass.

He looked like an old biker. His hair was grey and nearly shoulder-length, caught up at the back in a neat ponytail. He had a full grey beard and moustache, bright blue eyes behind rimless glasses, and what I interpreted as a hopeful grin. He was dressed in faded jeans and a brown leather jacket. I'd never seen him before. I pointed to the sign on the door which should already have told him, if he could read, 'TUESDAYS BY APPOINTMENT ONLY'. Then I smiled at him in a conciliatory way – after all, he *might* be a millionaire book collector even though he looked more like a superannuated hippy. I was turning away when he unfolded something he had been holding and pressed it flat against the glass. I saw the shape of an envelope and then the two second-class stamps, and I reached for the lock.

The man stepped inside. He said, 'Hey. I'm Ishmael Peters.' He made a little gesture, pushing the envelope toward me like a visiting card, and I took it and read that very name above an address in Amsterdam. My fingers bent the envelope just enough for me to check that there was still a sheet of paper inside, although the envelope had been opened. 'I got here last night, but it was too late to come around. I'm looking for Gabriel. I see he was here a coupla days ago.' He explained his certainty by nodding at the envelope that I was still clutching. The American accent was strong. 'He was supposed to be back on Thursday, Friday at the latest, but he didn't turn up, and his cell phone's been switched off all this time. I thought something must be wrong, so I came over through Harwich yesterday afternoon . . .'

I think my jaw had dropped. My heart certainly sank.

He was holding on to his smile now, because he must have seen something in my face. 'There's a paper in there, an agreement, between you and Gabe, and it's dated last Tuesday, that's why I came to see if you know where he is.'

Suddenly the day had turned darker. I said, 'You'd better come in.' And I brought him inside, shut the door behind him, tried to decide what to do, and bought a little time by saying, 'How do you know Gabriel?'

He said simply, 'We've been partners for the past coupla years. I've been in Amsterdam since 1970, and Gabe moved there a while ago so we could be together.'

30

What I most felt like doing was shrieking, 'Why me?' At that point I noticed Ernie across the road walking briskly in our direction, which would give me a few minutes to think about it. I leaped to reopen the door. As soon as he was in earshot I snapped, 'Hold the fort,' and pushed Ishmael into the office so I could shut the door behind us while I told him, watching his face. He was overweight, and I was thinking of heart attacks, but all he did was round his shoulders and lower his head. We sat in silence for what felt like hours, listening to the sounds of hard work from the shop and the traffic in the street outside.

'Would you like a drink?' I asked him when the silence had grown too heavy to continue.

He shook his bowed head, and muttered, 'If you've got . . . I wouldn't mind some coffee.'

I'd been thinking more along the lines of the bottle of Irish whiskey I always keep upstairs for my father, but coffee was just as easy, and I could use a caffeine jolt myself. I rinsed out a couple of the mugs sitting in the sink, shook them upside down, and found the jar of sugar on the shelf above.

'I could go and get some milk.'

He shook his head again. 'Black. Sure.'

I wondered whether he was crying. I said feebly, 'I'm sorry.'

'What . . .' he said. 'What happened?'

I'd been waiting for that. 'They don't know. He was lying beside the A12 near his bike. I don't know anything really, but there was an item in the local newspaper the next day, and a bookseller who lives near there reported it on an internet discussion group, a booksellers' list. That's how I found out. Can I ask you something?'

He seemed not to hear, but I persisted.

'I bought some books from him that same morning for cash. Well, you probably read that agreement he sent you. But the money wasn't on him when he was found. I think they'd like to know what happened to it. Do you know whether he still had a bank account over here?'

I didn't get a straight answer. Instead, after a moment, he

31

said, 'Do they think it was stolen? Is that why . . . ? You mean it wasn't an accident?'

*Careful!* I said, 'It might or might not have been. They don't really know . . .' I was interrupted by the ringing of the telephone, picked it up to stop the noise and said, 'I can't talk right now, could you . . .'

'Ms Hoare, it's DS Smiley.'

Oh. I looked at my visitor, looked away again and said, 'Hello.'

'Essex have been asking about you. I know it's a working day, but I wondered whether you could find a few minutes to come over here and get that statement sorted out.' Her tone said, 'and get them out of my hair.' I knew Smiley: we'd had business together a few months ago.

I said, 'Wait a second,' and covered the mouthpiece with my hand. It seemed sensible to say, 'It's the police. I'm supposed to be going over to the station to make a statement about seeing Gabriel that day. One of the things they were asking me is what happened to that agreement he sent you. Look, could you bear to come with me? We might be able to get the formalities over with, if you will, and they'll be able to tell you the things you want to know.'

He thought about it. 'They're investigating it?'

I nodded.

'They'll want to ask a lot of questions.'

I thought about that. 'Not really,' I said. 'These are the local police. Islington. They've just been asked to do the Essex police a favour by getting a statement from me. The people in Chelmsford are the ones who are investigating, and I'm sure they'll want to talk to you about Gabriel as soon as they can. But these people I'm supposed to see will phone Chelmsford and tell them you've turned up, and . . . It would be simpler, I guess.'

He said, 'Yeah.' It had a bitter edge. He clarified his meaning by nodding his head, and I removed my hand and told Smiley that I would be coming along with the dead man's partner, who happened to be with me at the moment and wanted to talk to them. Judging from the expression on his face, 'Wanted' wasn't quite the word, but it seemed tactful.

I did two things before we left. His envelope was lying on my desk. I picked it up and handed it to him slowly enough to be able to read the address twice and remember it until I could stroll casually over to the packing table, position myself behind his back, and scribble the details down on a scrap of wrapping paper, just in case. The second thing was to warn Ernie that I could be out for a while and ask him whether he was able to stay and then, when he told me that he had a class in an hour, to usher both him and our American visitor out, set the alarm and lock the door. My purple MPV was sitting across the street. I waved goodbye to Ernie, directed my silent companion into the front passenger seat, and took off.

# Headache

When I came back on my own an hour later, Barnabas was lying in ambush. I'd noticed a light on in the office just as I was unlocking the door, so I wasn't totally surprised to hear his voice from some spot in there saying, 'Dido, where did you go? What's this?'

'This' turned out to be the scrap of wrapping paper on which I'd scribbled Ishmael Peters's address.

'Ishmael Peters is Gabriel Steen's partner. He came over from Amsterdam yesterday, and he turned up here this morning.'

'Really? In the flesh?'

It sounded a strange question for him to ask, but I confirmed it – yes, quite a lot of flesh, I thought briefly.

'What's so funny?'

'Nothing,' I said quickly.

Barnabas was still frowning at the paper. 'The name,' he announced, 'seems familiar to me, and yet I can't think where I've heard it. Has he ever been to the shop before?'

I told him no, not as far as I could remember.

Barnabas wondered how he had known to come to me, and I explained that he had turned up with the missing envelope, and that what he was holding was the address I'd copied from that envelope. He put it down quickly. 'I suppose he came over because of Steen's death.'

'No. That was awful.' I told him exactly what had happened, and he unbent for a moment to pat my shoulder. 'And then Laura Smiley phoned: you know, the DS at the police station that I met last winter? She wanted me to go in and give them a statement about Gabriel's visit that they could fax to the Essex people. Mr Peters came with me.

34

It took me a little longer to finish over there than I'd expected, because they phoned Chelmsford on the spot, and there were a lot of explanations, and then they arranged to drive Mr Peters up there. He has to identify the body and – oh, talk to them, I suppose, about what Gabriel was doing here.'

My father gave my shoulder another pat and followed it with the suggestion that I'd had a hard morning and perhaps we should just go upstairs now and sit down with a cup of tea and talk things over.

I looked around. The shop was all right. The answering machine was sitting there, dark and hopeful, but I couldn't see anything that I needed to do for the moment. I did take that scrap of brown paper and push it down into a pocket of my jeans as we were leaving.

Barnabas replaced his empty cup on the low coffee table in front of the settee and said, 'They – the police, I mean – are behaving as though they know a good deal more about Gabriel Steen's death than they have made public.'

I wasn't going to argue: I'd been thinking something like that ever since I'd spoken to Quinn. But to be fair, I'd had a head start in the suspicion game, because I had guessed that something was wrong even before Gabriel had left me that other morning. I was beginning to wish I could believe he had simply been mugged and killed for the cash. That would be the easy answer, the safe one. Only it didn't allow for everything that had happened. He obviously hadn't turned up with the intention of selling me a share in the weird little manuscript. He hadn't even bothered to show it to me until after he'd received the phone call. The phone call was *why* he had shown it to me.

The phone interrupted us. I jumped, got hold of myself, and went to grab it.

'Dido, are you all right?' It was Chris Kennedy's voice, sounding a little anxious.

'Yes? Why not? Is something wrong?'

He laughed. 'No, it's just that you said you'd be in the

shop all day, and I got the answering machine twice when I phoned.'

I said slowly, 'I'm just fiddling around today,' not feeling quite easy about it. I added hastily, 'You forgot that I had to go over to the police station. It took longer than I expected because I had somebody with me. Gabriel Steen's partner turned up this morning. Chris, he hadn't heard. He was looking for Gabriel, because Gabriel was overdue, and I had to tell him.'

For the second time Chris said, 'Are you all right?'

I avoided giving him an answer by saying that Barnabas was with me, and the conversation wound down. I was just going to say goodbye when Barnabas shouted, 'Wait!' and removed the receiver from my hand.

'Hello,' I heard him say. 'Yes, thank you, yes. Yes, she is. I shall be here for most of the day in any case. Mr Kennedy, you could do me a favour if you would. Does the name Ishmael Peters mean anything to you? . . . Yes, Gabriel Steen's friend . . . No, but it is bothering me. I have the impression that I have heard the name before, and yet I can't imagine where, or why it would be familiar. A name like Ishmael of course . . . Thank you, I'd be very grateful.'

I said, 'Research?'

'You keep calling him an "investigative" journalist. In any case, he has promised to run the name through the computer at least, and ask the newspaper's librarian to help. I find this sense of familiarity, well, distracting. It's probably just a mistake. Some other similar name. The problem is, I find myself thinking about this kind of thing too much. Very annoying.'

Frankly, I thought that there were more important things to be thinking about. But I know how an unidentified memory, like an echo you can't pin down, keeps getting in the way of other things.

'It's nearly one thirty,' Barnabas observed. 'Should we eat? I could take you out to lunch.'

'I'll make some sandwiches,' I said. I realized that I was starting to be uneasy about being away from the shop for any time, as though something else or somebody else might turn up there unannounced and urgent. I was even thinking that I should go downstairs and clear up the rest of the book fair re-shelving job before that something else happened. I could feel a headache coming on.

# Heartache

I'd dealt with an e-mail from someone who had changed her mind about buying the Tennyson she'd turned down at the fair, wrapped that and two other small orders, asked my restless father whether he felt like taking a stroll over to the post office with them at some point, and was just shelving the last few books from the book fair when I saw Ishmael Peters outside on the pavement. I must have been waiting for something like that. We looked at each other through the glass of the door, and I let him in again.

He walked past me, eyes vacant, jaw set, and into the office where he dropped on to the visitor's chair. I hovered.

He said, 'It's my fault.'

I sat down opposite him, waiting.

Barnabas, who had been absorbed in something on the illustrated books shelves, had inched silently into the doorway. When Peters showed no sign of saying anything else, he cleared his throat.

'I'm Dido's father, Barnabas Hoare.'

Peters just scowled.

'Why do you say it was your fault? Do you think you could have prevented what happened to him? How on earth could you have done that?'

Peters managed to slump a bit lower. 'I shouldn't have let him come alone.'

Oh. So it was just the usual if-only-I'd-known. I glanced at Barnabas and found him staring with narrowed eyes at the top of Peters's head. I knew the look. He had probably practised it on a thousand students who had come to him with the excuse that the dog had eaten their essay.

'What did the police say?' Barnabas asked quietly. 'Do they know what happened yet?'

'They think that somebody did it. Killed him and got rid of him in a lay-by. Not an accident. They were doing a square dance, but that's what it comes to.'

He seemed to shake himself, and then looked at me.

I looked straight back and said, 'He took a call on his mobile while he was here with me. Do they know who that was?'

He shook his head promptly. 'Didn't say anything about that. Just . . . I said I'd come back for the inquest. They might need to ask me some questions. I'm on my way to the airport now. Going home. I came by here to ask you for the manuscript. I know you gave him a couple of thousand pounds, but I can give you that back. I'll send it as soon as I get home.'

My father really didn't need to intervene at this point, but he did anyway. 'My daughter says you have one copy of the document signed by herself and Gabriel Steen? If so, you know what the legal position is. He sold her the right to find a buyer for the manuscript in question, and specified the division of the proceeds. Would you be Mr Steen's heir?'

Peters looked at him without any expression. 'Yeah.'

'Then I can assure you that we are putting our best efforts into fulfilling the terms of the agreement. You – and any other heirs – can be sure of that. When the estate is settled, which I presume will be through the Netherlands legal system, will you kindly have them send us the documentation. And in the meantime, before you go, please leave your address in case we need to contact you.'

He pulled a sheet of paper out of the printer tray, placed it in front of our visitor, and offered him a ball-point from the holder.

Peters stared at the pen for a moment, gave a nod which wasn't much more than a twitch, and then scrawled what was required across the sheet. He added a long phone number and sat back looking at his hands.

'I'm so sorry,' I said softly. And I really was. I'd always liked Gabriel Steen.

Peters nodded at some point in the air between my father and me, lumbered to his feet and walked out. We watched him plodding back the way he had come, and Barnabas went and re-locked the door. While he was doing that, I read what Peters had written: 'Ishmael Peters, Reidsestraat 23, Amsterdam . . .' I opened my mouth, and closed it again because there could be any number of innocent reasons why this address was not the same as the one I had copied off Gabriel's envelope.

'I know that name,' Barnabas said decisively. 'This is really annoying.'

# Quinn

B y four thirty, the working day had stuttered to a close.
I'd even swept the floor of the shop and taken a sack
of rubbish out to the bin, and I could open for business in
the morning without actually repelling any customers. I
announced that I would go to the post office and then leave
early to pick Ben up, and Barnabas decided to come with
me as far as the bus stop. Everything went according to plan
until I was walking back towards the nursery school and
threw a glance to my left as I was crossing George Street.
There was an unfamiliar car sitting in front of the shop and
it looked as though an equally unfamiliar figure was standing
at the door and ringing the bell. I must have left a light on
in the office. Never mind: bringing Ben home took priority,
anything else could wait. Or preferably go away. I looked
straight ahead and picked up speed. But when we came back
half an hour later, talking about Ben's day, the car was still
there; and as we approached the door to the stairs leading
up to the flat, a man who had been standing in front of it
turned and walked towards us. He was holding out a little
folder holding the kind of identification which I recognized
even in the dim light from the street lamp.

'Miss Hoare? DI Quinn, from Chelmsford. I hope it isn't
inconvenient? I did leave a message on your answering
machine about an hour ago, but I wasn't far away so I thought
I'd drop by on the off-chance. I'd be grateful if you could
give me five minutes.'

The thought crossed my mind that he had spent a long
time standing outside the shop for somebody who had just
'dropped by' for no reason other than a five-minute chat.

I said, 'I'm going upstairs. I need to get my son's supper

ready.' But of course I couldn't just leave it there – I never can. 'You can come up if you want to.'

My kitchen is about the size of a big walk-in wardrobe. I settled Ben in his chair at one side of the tiny table, next to the wall, and our visitor in the second chair, which left me on my feet, leaning against the edge of the sink. Ben's attention moved between a plate of beef stew with chips and the face of our visitor. I noticed that my son's expression mirrored the kind of polite impatience that his grandfather normally shows whenever the police appear, a happening which Barnabas considers to be much too frequent. Maybe the two of them were starting to team up to keep an eye on my actions?

But I couldn't really see much wrong with Quinn, not yet. He was a solid man about my age, medium height, with short-cut brown hair, blue eyes, a quick smile, and a calm manner. He was sitting there politely with a mug of tea to hand and making small talk. I wondered whether he was taking things gently because of Ben. I threw a quick look at the hand which was cradling the tea, saw a wedding ring, and made a guess that he might have young children of his own. But I didn't see why we would be discussing any horrors here.

'*You* wanted to talk,' I pointed out. 'Can I help you with something?'

He looked at me keenly. 'I'm hoping so. We're having some problems with Gabriel Steen's accident. I read your statement and phoned DS Smiley. You know who I'm talking about?'

I said that I'd met her a few times.

'So she said. You told her that you'd known Gabriel Steen for quite a few years?'

I agreed and told him what seemed likely to be useful. A business relationship, satisfactory. 'I hadn't seen him for a while. Three years, maybe longer. I wasn't expecting him last week, and then he just turned up. He brought some books he thought that I might be interested in buying.'

He glanced down at his tea, and then up again. 'It's the cash that I was wondering about. Is it normal for you to

42

pay cash to somebody who comes in to sell you something?'

'Not that much cash,' I admitted, and then repeated my story of Steen's sudden change of direction and my purchase. He listened as carefully as though he hadn't heard all this before, though the formal statement I'd made had said exactly the same things.

'And you're pretty sure that all this happened because of the phone call he got?'

I was more than pretty sure. I told him that it had all seemed very clear to me at the time.

That was when he hesitated slightly and looked at me hard. I began to wonder whether somebody had been talking about me. Maybe he saw my uneasiness, because a momentary smile slid across his face. 'I don't suppose that anybody told you this, but he had about five pounds in loose change in his pockets when they found him, and a couple of tens in a billfold. That was all. Look, I'd be grateful if you could tell me whether you heard anything during this phone call that might help us to identify the caller or what they were talking about.'

'But I couldn't hear anything at all,' I explained. 'He answered the phone, and either he knew the voice or . . . no, I'm pretty sure it was that. But he went outside to talk. He only came back after the call was finished, and that's when he said he needed cash and showed me a manuscript that he'd brought with him.'

'And you bought it.'

'I bought a half share in it,' I said. I was getting uneasy at the way I was being asked to repeat things I'd already told them. I could see that he was doing this in order to check my story, to discover whether it would turn out to be exactly the same as the version I'd already given them. That made me defensive, and I said sharply, 'You can find out who the call came from, can't you? Would there be a record of the caller's number in the phone? It was somebody he knew, so their number is probably in his directory, anyway. Haven't you checked the numbers there? I can tell you one thing – the more I think about it, the more sure I am that it was somebody he knew.'

'We haven't found his phone.'

'It wasn't on his body?'

I received a shake of the head.

I covered my confusion by pouring us both a little more of the cooling tea and offering the milk. Ben stuffed his last two chips into his mouth and chewed, looked expectant, and received an apple from the fruit bowl on the counter. I was thinking that people don't just throw away their mobile phones. Losing one can seem like a catastrophe if you're in another country, cycling around from place to place.

I said, 'What about his rucksack?'

Quinn made a slight face at the taste of the stewed and cooling tea, set the mug down. 'That was there. Passport and a return ferry ticket in an outside pocket, plastic bag with dirty underwear in the bottom, a cleanish sweater, and half a dozen second-hand books. Anything ring a bell?'

I told him that I'd probably seen the books, and couldn't vouch for anything else. Dirty underwear? Thanks.

'And no cycling helmet,' I said softly. 'It couldn't have, I don't know, been overlooked in the grass where he was found, or something like that?'

Quinn shook his head. 'No. They searched the immediate area twice, in daylight. No.'

I hesitated, but he could only bite my head off. I said, 'So that's why you think he was murdered.'

Quinn leaned back in the chair and looked at me. I couldn't see any hostility there. 'We believe there's a good chance of it. When you told us about the helmet, alarm bells rang. The autopsy results had already raised some questions.'

I said, 'I know. I heard about that. He couldn't possibly have been hit by a car, you mean?'

'Possibly?' he repeated. 'It can't be ruled out. But that isn't what I meant. His body was found at about eight o'clock on Tuesday night. A lorry driver stopped in the lay-by just before eight. He was sitting up high, well above road level, of course, and just before he turned his headlights off he caught a glimpse of something in the ditch. He was curious about it, so he took his torch and got out to have a look. It turned out to be a bicycle lying just off the paved berm.

Steen was a bit further away, underneath some bushes. The driver called 999 on his mobile, and there was a patrol car only a mile or two away. They got there just on eight fifteen. We might have gone on thinking it was a straightforward traffic accident, except that some problems started to come up. And then we began to notice too many holes in the picture. And coincidences.'

'What kind of things?' I asked cautiously.

'One in particular. According to the autopsy findings, he must have died between about six and eight hours before he was found.'

It sounded as though I was being given an oral exam. I did the arithmetic. Between noon and two in the afternoon? I didn't understand at first, and I asked hesitantly, 'Could he have biked that far after he left me? I don't think that could have been later than eleven o'clock. How many miles is it?'

Quinn shrugged. 'It might be just about possible. He was riding a great bike – very fast. But he had a good section of London to get through, with all the traffic lights and whatnot. Not that cyclists necessarily pay much attention to minor details like lights. Then the A12 is pretty well built up until you get well outside the city, which means more traffic lights at the junctions, and lots of local stuff as well as the through traffic. He'd have had to be burning it the whole way. But that isn't exactly what I'm getting at. It gets dark by about five thirty these days, and the spot where he was lying had no road lighting or anything like that. But at midday? How could he possibly have been lying beside a busy road, and just off a lay-by that gets a lot of use for – what, at least three or four hours of daylight – and not be noticed by anybody?'

I thought about it. It wasn't possible. And if you put this problem together with the others, especially the missing helmet, it was enough to make anybody uneasy. Too many holes, too many questions.

'Why are you here?' I wondered aloud. 'I haven't really told you anything more to your face than I put in my statement, have I?'

I caught a flash of the grin again. 'I like being told things

45

to my face when an investigation's getting complicated. It makes it easier to know whether people are lying if you can watch their body language, believe me. Besides, I wanted to thank you for getting Ishmael Peters to talk to us. You saved us a lot of time, one way or another. Lucky he was travelling on a US passport.'

I said, 'I'll bite: why lucky?'

'Because there are immigration records at Gatwick. We were able to check that he really didn't get to England until after Steen was already dead.'

I shook my head. 'No, it wasn't him. He feels . . . He said to me that it was his fault it happened, and when I asked him what he was talking about, he said he should have been here with Gabriel. He came back to the shop after you'd talked to him, and he was miserable. Wiped out by what happened, I'd have said.'

'Mm. I had the same impression, though there was something else. I thought he was frightened.'

I was so surprised to find a policeman offering that kind of information to *me* that I almost missed the point of what he was saying. But when I thought about it, I knew he was right. I was turning that knowledge over and over in my head. Frightened? That could have been what I had seen in him.

When I came to, I found Quinn and Ben both looking at me hard.

'Frightened of what?' I quavered obligingly.

'Good question. I can't answer it. Do you think that you might be able to, if you thought about it some more?'

I had already thought. I asked, 'Frightened because he knew that Gabriel had been murdered, and because he's in the same kind of danger that Gabriel was?'

'I wondered about that. Can you think of anything that might give us the answer? Right now, I'd be grateful for anything, even a guess.'

But didn't think I could remember anything that I hadn't already told him. If the danger had to do with the manuscript, then why would Peters have wanted to risk taking it away with him? Better to sit and wait for me to make the sale and deliver a small fortune to him, free and without risk, surely? That was assuming that he had told me the truth and was in fact Gabriel's heir. Was he really so dim that he'd think I'd just take his word for it? Or on the other hand, did he just assume that I'd try to cheat him somehow? He knew from the agreement that Gabriel had trusted me, even if it hadn't occurred to him that I have a professional reputation to protect. Suddenly I needed to talk to Barnabas. We really had to find out just what was sitting in Leonard Stockton's safe.

'I'd better get off,' Quinn said abruptly. 'I have an hour's drive ahead of me, with the traffic the way it is at this time of day. If you think of anything else would you phone me? Don't hesitate. Anything.' He was sliding a card across the table which gave his name and rank and address, and phone numbers including his mobile. 'I can let myself out. I've taken up enough of your time already, and you'll want . . .' He threw a quick glance from me to Ben. Then he exchanged manly nods with Ben and gave me a long look. There was something in it that I couldn't read. I nodded and listened to him letting himself out of the flat and descending the stairs. The street door slammed, and after a minute or so a car started up outside and moved away. I was glad he'd gone. Though when I thought of it, I realized that he hadn't once told me to mind my own business. For a police officer, this had to be some kind of record.

# In Darkness

I woke up in darkness with the last vibrations of a bell still ringing in my ears. I waited for it to chime again, and when the silence was unbroken I turned on to my side to look at the time. Exactly four a.m. The bells in the big parish church a little to the south must have been what woke me. I considered the situation: it seemed my body had decided that six hours' sleep was enough, because I found myself feeling bright and much too wide awake.

The bedroom door creaked, and Mr Spock arrived, jumped on to the bed, and settled at my feet on top of the duvet. At the other side of the room, the sound of Ben's regular breathing came from the cot. Apparently I was the only one here who was feeling lively. Hot chocolate might fix that. I slid carefully out from under the covers and crept towards the hallway, turned right and tiptoed into the kitchen, where I could shut the door and turn on a light. I found the jar of chocolate, put some milk into the microwave to heat up, and stirred a couple of spoonfuls of the dark, rich shavings into the mug. Dark chocolate makes almost anything seem better. I sipped it while I stood and stared through the window at the backs of the big Victorian houses in the next street. There were one or two lonely lights in their back rooms, but mostly I was just looking at black shapes. There was no moon, and nothing moving.

Ishmael Peters. A man with two addresses. I wondered where he was sleeping tonight, if he was able to sleep. It would be past five o'clock in Amsterdam. Was he able to sleep?

Why did Barnabas think he had heard the name before?

*Dido, you are an idiot. You should have found that out by now.*

I'd have to leave Ben alone for ten minutes, so I crept back the way I'd come, slid into the bedroom, switched on the old baby alarm which was still sitting plugged in on the chest of drawers, even though it had been a while since I'd used it, and stuffed my bare feet into my trainers while I was at it. In the hallway, I slid into my coat, picked up my keys, listened again, and then let myself out slowly and silently. At the street door I repeated my stealth. It was only a few steps along the pavement to the door of the shop. I unlocked that, sped to the controls and turned off the alarm system, and then shut myself into the office before I turned on any lights. There was no sound coming from the baby alarm. I'd had the foresight to bring the mug with me, so I took another sip and switched on the computer. Five or six minutes later, after I had written down six lines of information on a memo pad, I switched it off again. There was a lot more left to look at, but I'd have to come back in the morning because I didn't want to do it now. The mug was empty and the hot chocolate was doing its work, because I yawned all the way up the stairs. Then I lay awake in bed after all, thinking about what I'd discovered.

When my father turned up at ten thirty, I was downstairs. The little Nepalese bells jangled as he opened the door, and I looked up from my place at the desk and checked in the mirror that was angled to give me a view of the entrance and the aisle immediately in front of it. It was intended to allow me to keep an eye on potential shoplifters, and also to identify my regular customers so that I could rush out to greet them. There had been no customers yet today.

Barnabas paused just inside the door, glanced around sharply, then fixed his gaze on the mirror, which would be showing him my reflection staring back at him. He was wearing an ancient mackintosh, with a sober dark-green muffler wound around his neck. The day was fine, but there was a cold easterly wind blowing, as I'd discovered when Ben and I had headed into it for the walk to nursery, and his cheeks and nose were pink.

'Barnabas, there's some fresh coffee.'

His reflection nodded at me, and then disappeared and reappeared in the flesh around the end of the bookcases nearest to the office door.

'And I've found out about Ishmael Peters. He's an artist.'

'He's a painter,' Barnabas agreed. 'It came to me as I was getting ready for bed last night. Ishmael Peters . . . there was an exhibition in Oxford. I recall a rather large banner with his name on it, strung over the entrance. Dear heavens! Your mother took me along to it. This was – oh, nine or ten years ago at least, I'd say. Before she was so ill. I can't remember much about his work. A little surrealistic, I seem to recall. With animals. Or . . . people-animals.'

I nodded smugly. 'He even sold something called "Deceitful Jaguars" to a big museum in Boston. I've been looking him up. Do you want to see?'

I made room for him at the computer, delivered half a mug of coffee to a spot well to the side of the keyboard, and took my time pouring my own and shuffling some invoices while Barnabas pointed and clicked with the mouse and scanned an assortment of old reviews, notices, potted biographies of the artist, and finally even a website from which Mr Peters was offering a selection of his works, with small images of each item on offer, short descriptions and prices that ranged from three hundred to fifty-five thousand euros.

I looked over his shoulder and waited for his reaction.

'He has a studio,' Barnabas muttered, 'and what seems to be some kind of permanent exhibition there. Or he did at one time – I can't see any indication of a date here.'

'It gives the postal address,' I pointed out. 'It's the address that he left when he was here, so it should be current.'

My father barely acknowledged this information, because he had clicked on About the Artist and was scanning the information there. '1970,' he said pointedly and then explained it by reading the passage aloud:

Ishmael Peters was born in New Haven, Connecticut, and studied at Yale University. In 1970 he moved to Canada and in the next year to Paris,

France. He has resided ever since in France and
the Netherlands where he has worked with . . .

'You realize,' Barnabas interrupted himself, 'what that's
about? The man was a Vietnam War refusenik. Many of them
fled to Canada to avoid military service. Conscription. They
were all pardoned at some point, but apparently Peters
preferred to stay abroad rather than go home.'

The thought came impatiently. That's old history.

I said quickly, 'I think I've noticed something about this.
There's not a lot of information from the past five years,
unless you've found something I didn't. No exhibitions, no
reviews or awards. Of course, he's an old man, so I suppose
he's more or less retired.'

'He would have been born in 1948 or '49, give or take,'
Barnabas said acidly. 'Not what I would describe as *particularly* old. He is apparently still selling his work, if his website
is to be believed.'

I shrugged. It didn't mean that he was making anything
new. I could imagine an impoverished artist with unsold
work from three previous decades trying to earn a little by
selling off the old paintings and prints. I had been married
to an artist for a couple of years, which incidentally did not
encourage me to trust artists much, and I could still remember
the unsold boards and canvases that had leaned six or seven
works deep around the edges of our rooms.

'Well,' my father said dismissively, 'perhaps you're saying
that I can forget about him now and concentrate on the manuscript? Unless you've miraculously discovered the nature of
that work? I have an appointment in an hour with somebody
at the British Library. I don't know how long I shall be. Are
you . . .?'

'Ernie is coming in at lunchtime,' I told him. I didn't add
that I had nothing to do until then. No business. Maybe a
visit to the launderette would be a good way to waste a couple
of hours? That notion rang a bell: clothes, laundry, pockets.

I said, 'I'll be back in a second. Just popping upstairs for
some fresh milk.' And I made a business of grabbing my
keys and rushing out.

51

My errand upstairs was with the laundry rather than anything in the fridge. I scrabbled through the clothes in the hamper beside the bathtub, located the jeans I had been wearing until this morning, and dug a slip of wrapping paper out of the pocket, the paper that contained my scribbled note of the address to which Gabriel Steen had posted that envelope. I hadn't misremembered anything. The address on it had been I. Peters, Marnixstraat 113. Not Reidsestraat. So Ishmael did have two addresses. Nothing wrong with that, of course, unless maybe he had left his business address, but not this other one, with the police as well as with me. Maybe he was just a very private person. Or maybe he had something to hide.

Mr Spock sauntered into the bathroom at that moment and pointed his noise at the pile of dirty laundry with what looked like a supercilious air. What dirty beasts these humans are.

# He Wants Something

The phone in the sitting room started to ring just as I was turning the sausages over in the frying pan. I slid the pan off the burner and went to answer it, glancing in on Ben, who was in the bedroom talking to Mr Spock, as I passed the door. It was a one-way conversation, as far as I could hear.

I was just hoping that this wasn't more bad news.

I didn't recognize the voice at first, but it soon enlightened me. 'Miss Hoare, this is Alan Quinn. I hope you don't mind me phoning you at this number, but I knew you'd be upstairs by this time. I wanted to thank you for your help on Tuesday. I appreciated it.'

My ears pricked up. I thanked him for thanking me, and said, 'I didn't realize that you had this number. It isn't listed.'

He said, 'Well, we have ways.' Yes, naturally: policeman talking. 'The thing is, I was wondering whether you'd heard from Mr Peters again.'

I opened my mouth, closed it again while I considered the question and then answered literally, 'No. Why?'

'I want to have another word with him, when I can find him. I've been told that there was a fire in his studio yesterday. The Amsterdam police would like to talk to him about it, and they asked me to find out whether he's still here.'

'Badly damaged?'

'The whole building was gutted. It was at night, luckily, and the caretaker got out before he was hurt, but several businesses were destroyed and I think they have some questions for him over there. It was arson, there's no doubt about that. If he's here, they want him to go back.'

'He didn't live in the studio?' I asked craftily. 'They're sure he's . . . you know . . . safe?'

'No, no, they're sure of that. The caretaker told them Peters was living somewhere else, but he wasn't very clear about where. Someone else in the building suggested that he was staying with Gabriel Steen. The police looked in Steen's flat, but nobody's there now.'

I adjusted the facts just a little by saying, 'Well, maybe that explains it. When I saw him before, he told me that he was flying home; but then this afternoon I thought I saw him across the street, but he didn't come in.'

'He hasn't contacted you at all?'

He hadn't, exactly, but I decided to mention that I'd had a silent phone call. Not that it necessarily meant anything.

'Right,' he said quietly. 'If he does phone you . . .'

'I'll tell him that you want to speak to him, and I'll try to get the number of the phone he's using and let you know,' I promised. 'I wish I knew why he's hanging around – if it *was* him.'

'He wants something from you,' Quinn suggested. 'You don't know what it is?'

'I'll think about it,' I said. Not that I had to. I was pretty sure by this time that I knew.

We said goodbye and I sped back to the kitchen, where the sausage fat was starting to coagulate, and got supper back on course. Then I rang Ernie's mobile.

His voice rolled through the earpiece with a cheerful 'Hello, Dido. What's up?'

'Problems,' I told him. 'I'll explain when I see you, but that's what I'm calling about. I need to be out of the shop a lot of the time for the next few days, and it would be really good if you could work some extra hours. What do you think?'

There was a short silence. In the background, I could hear voices and traffic noises. 'I'm lookin' at my timetable. I can come in tomorrow after my first class, and stay the.afternoon, an' Saturday as usual.'

It was going to cost me a mint, and I didn't care. If I could speak to Ishmael Peters, I thought I'd probably be able to find out what he was really up to and decide whether I needed to do anything about it. Until that happened, I'd at least make

54

sure that I had some company while I was in the shop. Barnabas might come in for some of the time, but I knew he had been out a lot during the last week or so, presumably in connection with the manuscript, and I didn't want to enlighten him about any of this unless it became necessary. For one thing, my father would probably insist on moving in here with us 24/7. So when I had to be on my own, I'd rather just close the shop and come upstairs to lurk and watch in case Peters came back. I probably wouldn't have too long to wait, because I was sure that I knew what he wanted to talk about.

# Surveillance

I was lying on the settee in the sitting room. I had the television on with the sound turned down to a whisper. I wasn't paying much attention to the programme, which was one of those things about people renovating their houses. There've been a lot of those recently and they bore me rigid. Instead, I was pondering the knowledge that I wasn't much enjoying the experience of lying around doing nothing. Since Ernie had turned up an hour ago to take care of the shop, I'd been up here trying not to fall asleep. From time to time I'd dragged myself to look furtively out of the window, keeping a kind of periodic watch on the street but there had been nobody hanging about and nothing much to look at.

It was nearly three when the phone rang. Earlier I'd brought it over and left it on the carpet in front of the settee, and as I felt for it hastily, knocked the receiver off, grabbed it and said, 'Hel—' just as Ernie's voice interrupted: 'Is this the one?' and then the connection was broken. I fell on to the floor, scrambled up, and leaned on the window sill, but I was too late to see anybody when I craned and peered down toward the shop door. I gritted my teeth, grabbed my jacket, and shot out of the room and down the stairs. At the bottom, I opened the street door a crack. A woman was pushing a stroller along the far side of the street, but she was the only person I could see. I decided to creep along the front of the shop and peek through the display window, but I'd barely stepped on to the pavement and shut the door when I heard the shop door opening and a voice. I just had time to duck into the little triangular space at the side of my building and crouch behind the wheelie bin before footsteps approached. Peters passed six feet from me, luckily without looking my way. He was wearing a dark-green duffel coat, and his head was bowed. He looked utterly miserable. I gave him just enough time to turn right into the cross street, and then I was shooting along the display window and bursting into the shop.

'Ernie! Listen, that *was* him! I'm going to see where he's heading. If I'm not back by four thirty, and I haven't phoned, will you go and pick Ben up? I'll be as quick as I can.'

Ernie started to ask me something, but there was no time to listen. I slammed the door and sprinted along to the corner. Ishmael Peters's grey head was still in sight, but by now he was passing the last shop before the pub on the corner of the main road. He then turned right and vanished. I ran for it. I was half expecting to see him disappearing into another taxi, but he was still there after all, plodding northwards past the little shops, not looking at the display windows, going somewhere. I am short enough to be hard to see in a crowd, so I trotted after him and closed some of the gap, stepping sideways behind a sheltering back whenever he appeared to hesitate, and keeping as many people as I dared between the two of us. But he showed no sign of knowing I was there. At the pedestrian lights near the Almeida Theatre, he turned and crossed to the west side of the road. I had no choice but to step back and wait. It seemed to take forever for the green man to start walking again. But I had seen Peters turn into a side street, and when the traffic stopped I ran across blindly and bounced off someone who was coming the other way in a hurry. I babbled an apology without stopping. I was starting to wish I'd sent Ernie to do this instead of me.

But the pavement at the side street was much clearer, and I could slow down again and let him get fifty metres ahead. I kept my eyes focussed on the grey ponytail, and saw him stop and turn to his left. He was climbing a short flight of steps to one of the doors up there, and after a moment's pause he vanished. I pushed myself into another trot. I hadn't been able to tell which of the doors he had entered, as the whole street was lined with terraces of identical four-storey mid-Victorian houses. But when I got to the spot I discovered that one of the doors had a discreet painted sign above the lintel which announced that it was the 'Nayland Hotel', and a small placard in its window proclaiming, 'Vacancies'. I followed the instructions on the little sign above the doorbell and rang it.

The door was opened by a thin blonde girl in a grey tracksuit with a name tag pinned to it. Katerina. Peters hadn't got very far yet, hesitating at a flight of stairs that led up from the wide entrance hall, and looking back at the open door.

I smiled and nodded at Katerina and called over her shoulder, 'Hello! I thought that was you I saw heading this way! Why don't we go and get a coffee? There's a place just along on the corner of the main road.'

Peters looked at me silently, with a face that was absolutely blank. After a moment, he nodded and started back down.

# Coffee and Conversation

The coffee shop is one of a chain which offers variations on the theme of strong-with-fizzed milk. I like them. We queued at the counter. He ordered espresso, I got a mocha. I paid, and he went ahead of me to take a seat at a four-person table tucked underneath the flight of wooden, open-tread stairs leading to the floor above. If he had been a little taller he would have had to slump in his chair to keep from banging his head. I'm five foot four, so low ceilings don't bother me. Or low staircases. The place was nearly full, but the feet which from time to time climbed the steps a few inches above our heads probably just discouraged anybody else from sharing our table, which suited us both.

We stared thoughtfully at one another. He wasn't going to help me: I decided to attack.

'I just hate getting silent phone calls,' I told him, keeping my tone casual.

He blinked and turned a little pink. Bingo! I sipped at my chocolate-flavoured froth while I looked at him and waited.

'I'm sorry. I wasn't sure what to do.'

'Say hello?'

He gave the obligatory short laugh. 'No, I mean, I needed to speak to you, but then it got a bit difficult, I guess.'

'Why "difficult"? I'm not the police! Talking about "difficult", I hear that the Essex police do want to speak to *you* urgently. They've been asking if I knew where you were. You had a fire? It's lucky that you weren't at home at the time.'

He shook his head impatiently. 'That was my business address. I don't live there at the moment. Didn't. Look—'

'Did you lose much stock?' I interrupted sympathetically.

'That's where you kept all your pictures? It must be horrible to lose your work like that.'

He looked at me. The corners of his mouth turned down grimly. 'It is. Pictures, all my materials.' He broke off and seemed to be lost in a memory. He scowled.

'Anyway,' I said soothingly, 'it's DI Quinn who was looking for you. I guess he must have given you his phone number when he saw you? Or – I've stored it in my mobile phone. Wait a minute.'

I pulled my phone out of my pocket, unlocked the keys, and found the number. He pulled a moleskin notebook out of a breast pocket and copied it as I read it out, then gulped half of his coffee. When he put the cup back into the saucer, his hand was shaking. I couldn't understand what was bothering him, so I just pretended not to notice. Maybe I should let up for a while.

'You should just have made an appointment,' I said casually. 'What did you want to talk to me about?'

I told myself, *Don't, don't let him say what I think he's going to say.* I thought that Peters probably wouldn't grant me my wish.

'It was arson,' he said, unexpectedly. 'One of the guys in the building had my cell phone number, and he phoned to tell me about it. I called the police in Amsterdam. They say somebody broke in during the night and set light to my stock of frames and boards. You see, I wanted to tell you that.'

'Is it connected with what happened to Gabriel?'

I caught a reluctant nod.

'Somebody from over in the Netherlands followed him here? Why?'

'You know why. Don't you?'

I wanted him to say it.

'Don't you see it's all about Gabe's manuscript?'

'They want to steal it?' I followed that train of thought. 'But if they thought that might be hidden in your studio, why would they risk setting a fire there?'

'It was a warning,' he said stubbornly. The message his body was giving out was that he knew, and I didn't, and he was kindly enlightening me. So I opened my mouth to say that this made no sense and changed that to a non-committal 'Oh.'

'And, Miss Hoare: if they know that you've got it, why won't they do it to you too? You wanna see your bookstore going up in flames?'

'I have a fire alarm,' I told him – I thought it was a good idea to let him know about it before he got out the matches. 'Maybe I should sell the book to these people for a lot of money.'

'How much?'

'What?' This was getting surreal.

'How much would you ask for it?'

I bought myself a moment by tipping up the cup and letting the last dregs of chocolate-flavoured coffee trickle into my mouth. Then I decided to tell him the truth: 'I don't know, because I still don't know what it is. And I need to make sure it's genuine. When I find that out, then I'll look at auction records and some websites and make up my mind what it's worth. Then I'll be able to offer it to any of my customers who are interested in that sort of thing. If that doesn't work, I'll advertise. If I can't do it that way, then I might send it to one of the big auction houses. But that takes time, and the cut that the auction house takes is pretty big, so I'll sell it privately if I can. That's how the antiquarian book business works.'

'Do you want another one?'

It took me a moment to understand that he had changed the subject, then I nodded and said, 'Thanks,' and watched him head back to the counter. I half expected him to take the chance to cut and run, but he came back in a couple of minutes with our repeat orders and settled down, looking determined.

'What if I buy it from you now, without all the fuss? How much would you want?'

'Two hundred thousand pounds, cash.'

He was silent for a moment. Then he laughed. Actually, it was more like a falsetto giggle. 'You're kidding?'

I said, 'No.'

'You have to be kidding me.'

'That's what I'd take if I had to sell it now for some reason.'

'So,' he said slowly, 'you really think it's worth that much?'

I said honestly, 'I don't know about that. It might be. But I don't know what it is yet. What can you tell me about it?'

He just shook his head and looked down at his hands, which were resting on the table.

'Didn't Gabriel ever say anything to you about it?'

'Oh, sure he did. He talked about it a lot for a while; he was going crazy about it. But if he had any ideas, he didn't tell me what they were.'

'When did he find it?'

His eyes skittered up at my face. 'I don't know. Some time last year.'

I persisted, 'He found it in a street market?'

'That's right. On one of his trips. He was trying to identify it, but no luck.'

'Why did he bring it to London? Had he found a buyer here?'

He twitched impatiently. 'Look, I don't know anything. He might've. Or maybe it was something else. If you want my guess, I mean, there's lots of people and museums in London, and a big university. It might be the nearest place to Amsterdam where he'd find so many experts, and he knew who they were because he used to live here. He wanted to know where the thing came from and what it was, and it was all a big blank to him. A mystery. He needed some help.'

That could make sense, especially since I was in exactly the same position. I asked the obvious question: 'Did he tell you anything about who he was coming to see? Any names?'

'Can't help you there. We'd got sorta tired of talking about it, frankly. We looked at it a lot, when he first got it, but neither of us could make any sense of something that old. It's really old, isn't it? He might have been getting impatient.'

'Did he think that somebody had found out about it and wanted to steal it?'

'He would've told me if it was that.'

'All right,' I said. 'I'm just wondering . . . why would somebody burn your place out? How does that connect? Did they think the manuscript was there? Why? Did Gabriel ever store some of his things in your studio?'

'Sure. We had more room for book stock there. He had a couple of sections of shelving he used. You know how books pile up.'

I did. I knew something else: if anybody really thought that a valuable manuscript was being kept there, why would they set a fire? They might do it to hide the fact that they'd stolen it, only they *hadn't* stolen it: Gabriel had taken it away with him, and now I had it. It made absolutely no sense, and I certainly couldn't ask this man to help me work it out because the only reason he was telling me this fairy tale had to be to confuse me.

'Well then,' I said with a sigh, 'lucky he hadn't left it there after all. And of course you're right, London is a good place to ask questions about that kind of thing.'

'So what are you going to do?'

'I will find out about it, sooner or later,' I promised him. Or maybe it was a promise to myself. 'And then I'll sell it for an appropriate price. But while I still don't know, then the whole thing is just one big guess, and I don't do business that way.'

'What if they come here looking for it?'

Oh-ho. I stared at him coldly and said, 'Why would anybody do that? Why would they think it's here? Are you saying you'd tell them I have it? Do you know who they are?'

I saw the embarrassment creep into his face. 'Of course not! What do you think?' But something was still flickering there. 'You said you'd have to advertise it, remember? Talk to people about it? They'll hear.'

'Really? So these arsonists are people in the book trade?'

He was sulking now like a little boy. 'They'd find out. I don't know how they'd do it, they just would.'

I looked at him. He looked down at the table top and was silent. I looked at the table to see what he was looking at, but it remained doubtful. I felt trapped there with nothing left to say, and had to struggle to pull myself together.

'Mr Peters, how long are you going to be in London?'

63

He shrugged. 'Who knows?'

I said, 'I have to go now. I have an errand to do. Don't forget about phoning Inspector Quinn. He might have some news for you from Amsterdam.' I gathered my jacket from the back of my chair and started to pull it on. Not looking at him, I added, 'If you let me know how to contact you in Amsterdam, I'll keep you up to date about the sale.'

'I'm not sure. I have to look for a place to live. I have to get busy on the legal stuff. Inventory, insurance claims, that kind of thing. I'm travelling back tomorrow morning.'

'And if you find anything about the manuscript, about what it is, among Gabriel's things, phone me about that too. I don't want to make any mistakes with this. If you're really his heir, you should remember I'm working in your interests as well as mine.'

'I know,' he said. 'I understand that. I'll go back to the hotel and call that cop now. Unless you want me to walk you back to the book store?'

I threw a look at my watch, which warned me that it was nearly five o'clock, and said, 'Actually, I'm going to have to go somewhere else first. Keep in touch, though. You've got the phone number. Don't forget – tell me anything you can find out about the manuscript. My researcher is still having some problems with it, I think.'

'The black guy I talked to in your store?'

'No, somebody else is dealing with the research side,' I told him. It sounded as though I had a large staff, which I thought would be a good message to get across. If Ishmael was right that somebody might turn up carrying a box of matches, I wouldn't mind having him think that a staff of hundreds, some of them armed, would be lurking in the shadows.

We left together, but I crossed the road and headed toward the nursery school. Half of me wanted to follow Peters, just to make sure that he really was heading back to the hotel and not going to meet some sinister-looking, flame-thrower-carrying Dutchman. It was a temptation, but impractical.

# Not Going Anywhere

When the phone rang, I picked it up carelessly without remembering that I was worried about who and what I would hear. In the event, it was my father's voice.

'Dido? I need to see you.' He sounded brisk.

'What's wrong?'

'Wrong? Nothing that I can put my finger on, but then nothing is precisely right, either.'

'How's it going?' I asked, sure that he'd know what I was talking about.

'It's not going well. It's not going anywhere. That's what I'm saying, and it is basically what I wish to discuss. But when I phoned the shop a couple of hours ago I found myself speaking to Ernie. I gather something has happened?'

It was definitely an accusation.

I told him that Ishmael Peters was back and realized I would have to outline the day's events, but barely got started.

'Stay where you are,' he said. 'I'll be there shortly.'

Ben was in bed, though not yet asleep; I could still hear him talking to himself in the darkened room. I had fed both him and Ernie an hour ago, and Ernie had gone away with another handful of cash to meet his mates from the university. Friday night is pub night in London. I had no plans apart from finding myself some food and slumping in front of the television while I tried to think through some of the things that had happened. Barnabas's visit suited this scheme. My father is very good at putting the elements of a puzzle together and coming up with an overall view. Very often he has turned out to have the right answers. I could use his help.

'Have you eaten?' was his final question.

I confessed that this was something I hadn't managed to find the time for.

'Don't,' he said. 'I shall bring something when I come. Give me half an hour.'

He hung up without waiting for me to accept his offer, and I went to wash my face and brush my hair. Then I looked critically at my reflection in the bathroom mirror. I could see that I needed a haircut and a bath, not necessarily in that order, and some sleep. My eyes were bloodshot, and I seemed to be developing little vertical lines between my eyebrows from too much thinking – or maybe frowning in bewilderment.

My father's habit is to give a quick ring at the doorbell and then let himself in and come upstairs. I trotted down the corridor when the bell sounded and opened the door of the flat to find him laden with two pizza boxes, his old brief-case, and a carrier bag containing a bottle. I stepped back hastily and closed the bedroom door, then made shushing gestures as he arrived on the landing.

Barnabas ignored them. 'Dido, I don't suppose that Mr Kennedy is here? While I was waiting for the food, it occurred to me that he might be able to help with something.'

I shook my head, waved him into the sitting room, and left him starting to unpack two medium pizzas and a bottle of red wine while I slid into the kitchen to locate knives and plates, two wine glasses (which needed to be washed and dried), a corkscrew and a roll of paper towels in place of napkins. When I returned to distribute these things, I found the food boxes sitting on the chair in front of the writing desk, and the wine bottle on the floor. The top of the coffee table, from which I'd intended us to eat, was covered with the photos of the manuscript folios which Barnabas had been carrying around. He was hanging over them, frowning and muttering to himself. I suffered from a sudden grave hunger pang and any discussion would have to wait until the pizzas had been divided into big segments and we were deep into four kinds of melted cheese with slices of spicy sausage or aubergine and artichoke.

When my mouth was empty for a second I plunged in, 'How old is that thing?'

Barnabas said, 'I don't know.' He made it sound like some kind of achievement. 'I ought to, but I don't.'

'And it's definitely not just some kind of mediaeval script that you aren't familiar with?'

'Not according to the Reader in Early English at University College.'

'Some other European language? Gabriel told me he'd found it in Italy.'

'That's not the issue,' Barnabas assured me. 'If this is a cipher, it could be any language. The script itself is another problem. Too many of the letters have no obvious latinate precedent. In other words, they are not European letters.'

There was one other possibility that occurred to me. 'So this is an invented alphabet, not just a code?' I reached for the last piece of the four cheeses pizza, caught myself and offered it to my father, then grabbed it as soon as he shook his head. My favourite.

'I know something about codes,' Barnabas pointed out mildly – and in fact unnecessarily, because he had worked as a code-breaker at Bletchley Park as a very young man during the Second World War. 'I am quite sure it is not just a simple substitution code. You understand? It does not simply substitute an . . . er . . . squiggle of a certain shape for the letter "a", and so forth. One would have to recognize the amount of work involved here. And one would certainly wish to ask why somebody would go to such trouble and what the connection might be between a coded text and the very interesting drawings. To be honest, I still have no idea.'

'What next, then?' I asked. I wanted to ask, *And what's brought you around here this evening?* There was obviously something still to come.

'Next,' Barnabas told me firmly, 'I shall pursue the question of the manuscript itself: the materials which have been used, the vellum, the ink . . . But I have looked at a thirteenth-century manuscript in the British Library, something called the *Ars Notoria*, which has the same mixture of illustrations – angels, astronomical figures, plants – as in our book. If I am right, the subject of Mr Steen's volume is magic. You understand what I'm saying?'

I thought fast. Magic. Thirteenth century. Roman Catholic church. 'You mean, it might have been something that had to be kept secret? Something dangerous?'

'That occurred to me. But we must take this carefully, not leap to false conclusions. The next step, as I just said, is to investigate the actual materials used. So I dropped by Leonard Stockton's office this afternoon and told him that I wanted to take it away for a short time, and he pointed out, quite correctly I'm sure, that you are his client and it would require your permission. Therefore in the morning, if you would phone Mr Stockton and tell—'

'No. No way!' I said, and scraped up a dribble of cheese from the bottom of one of the boxes, pretending not to notice the look on my father's face. I sucked up the cheese, picked up my glass with the last half inch of wine in it, emptied it, and said, 'Ishmael Peters is back in London. He's been here for a couple of days, and I think he's phoned me a couple of times, though he never says anything, or leaves a message, and he doesn't really have a story to explain things. He came to the shop this afternoon and spoke to Ernie. I think what he wants is to get the manuscript back. I had a long and weird talk with him, and there were all kinds of holes in his story, but there is definitely something going on. Do you want to hear about it?' It was a rhetorical question.

When I'd finished giving him as much detail as I could remember, Barnabas stared at me. 'What? There has to be more.'

'He said that there is somebody who wants the manuscript. Or wants it back, I wasn't sure which. Maybe he stole it from them. He said that this person set the fire that destroyed his studio. I pointed out it was a crazy thing to do if they thought it was hidden there, which what he'd been hinting, and then he backed down. He just didn't make any sense. He said that "they" would find out I had it, and they'd come and get it. He claimed he was doing me a favour by taking it away.'

'And you said . . . ?'

'That it wasn't in the shop, it was locked up in a vault, that I had bought the right to sell it and take a share of the

68

price, and that this is exactly what I intend to do. He seemed to accept that, but he didn't like it.'

When I looked up, I noticed that Barnabas was scowling. I shook my head. 'He's a bit emotional, but I'm not afraid of Ishmael Peters! In fact, I think he's pathetic.'

'And long may you continue to think so,' my father growled. 'All the more reason to go to work and then take the thing off your hands. There is quite a simple way to do that, you know. Ideally, it would involve transporting the thing down to Sotheby's or Christie's by security van, first thing in the morning, and getting them to list it in the next appropriate book auction.'

'And then somebody could burn down the auction house instead of the shop. Or the auction house could take one look at it and have me arrested very publicly for handling stolen property.' It was just a suggestion, but it looked as though he understood my point.

Barnabas took charge. He removed a pen from the pocket of his sports jacket, helped himself to a sheet of paper from the pad sitting on the writing desk, and said, 'Dido, I want you to go through your conversation with Peters again. Tell me everything that he said about the manuscript and about this mysterious criminal who is looking for it. I agree that it is *not* the most logical tale I have ever heard. If you start at the beginning, perhaps . . .? That would be Gabriel Steen's visit. Tell me again about the sequence of events the day Steen brought it here, with as much detail as you can manage about Peters. Take your time.'

I looked at the clock on the shelf above the fireplace. It was only eight fifteen, so I could not excuse myself and go to bed for at least another hour. Anyway, I knew what I had to do.

'Gabriel,' I said, 'turned up to offer me some books. Nineteenth-century English, Beardsley engravings, nothing unusual. He didn't show me the manuscript at first, but then something happened – a call came on his mobile phone. When he had finished taking it, I could see that he'd had some disturbing news.'

Even with Barnabas's questions, the story took no more

than twenty minutes, and that included the interludes when he stopped to make notes of every hole he could see in my tale. He finished by listing the problems to be solved.

'And he was killed within an hour, or thereabouts, of the time he left you?'

'Well,' I said, 'apparently it isn't a very precise thing, but the police say that's about right.'

'You're getting on with this detective, Quinn?'

'He seems all right,' I conceded. 'He acts like a human being. He hasn't told me to mind my own business. Yet.'

'Has he behaved improperly?' Barnabas enquired.

I made him a really-shocked face.

'Has he given you any information that he shouldn't?' My father sighed pointedly. I shook my head. 'Then that's probably all I can think of at the moment. Dido, I have a suggestion. Will you contact Mr Kennedy in the morning and ask him to talk to this detective and find out whatever he can about Steen, and Ishmael Peters, and what happened in Amsterdam? Meanwhile, I have come to a decision. Considering everything, the next step must be to identify the manuscript. I think I must take it somewhere. I have been in touch with a man in the manuscripts section at the British Library, someone whom I've known for several years. He has agreed to help with a thorough physical analysis of the book. It will be stored under lock and key, and I truly can't imagine it being less secure there than it is in Mr Stockton's safe.'

I nodded. I was half expecting him to shout, 'To horse!' In fact he lapsed into silence and scribbled several more unreadable notes to himself.

'And what am I supposed to do?' I asked sweetly.

'Run a business?' Barnabas suggested. 'And – if Mr Spock's pacing and glaring is telling us anything – feed the cat.'

All right. Fine with me. It suited me right down to a T. No more chasing dubious characters through the streets, or worrying about mad visitors, or sinister shadows or . . .

'And I think it would be wise to have Ernie about the place as much as possible when we are open, don't you?'

he went on, spoiling the mood. 'Aside from that, perhaps you should have an early night, and then contact both Chris and Mr Stockton in the morning.'

'Tomorrow is Saturday,' I reminded him. 'I can get hold of Chris, but Mr Stockton might not be in his office.'

Barnabas sighed. 'Of course, you're right. So I shall be here by ten o'clock and we will open the shop together. Stay upstairs with Ben until I arrive.'

I crammed two handfuls of dirty plates, the empty wine bottle and paper rubbish into my father's carrier bag and headed wordlessly toward the kitchen. And the tin opener. Maybe I *was* growing old and forgetful. Mr Spock followed very close on my heels.

# Distraction

By mid-morning on Saturday the shop was almost crowded. Ben and I were taking up most of the free space in the office. He was flicking through a picture book he had brought downstairs with him while I was flicking through the pages of two book catalogues which had arrived with the morning's post, so far without much excitement. Admittedly I was finding it hard to concentrate. I realized that every time the street door opened, I was craning to see whether the wrong kind of person had come in. Ernie sat at the computer, busy making some unspecified changes to our website. Barnabas had been driven out of the office by the overcrowding and was circulating among the bookshelves, offering help to anyone who asked and a few people who didn't; this morning there was actually a thin but steady stream of customers.

When the phone rang, Ernie happened to be nearest. He picked it up and I heard him start to say, 'Dido Hoare Antiqu— Oh . . . Yeah, she's here.' He placed the receiver at the edge of the desk nearest to where I sat, and I scooped it up gingerly.

'Hello?'

'Dido? It's Chris. Can you talk now?'

I said, 'It's busy here, but yes, for a moment. Any luck?'

'Maybe. There's something interesting, anyway. Look, what about lunch?'

I told him that I wasn't sure I could get away, or that I could be absent for too long, and that Ben would be with me if it did prove possible.

I had begun my day three hours earlier by ringing Chris Kennedy on his mobile and waking him up to tell him about

72

the events of the last couple of days. Especially about Ishmael Peters's return to London, and what he had said about the fire and the manuscript and the possibility of a threat. Chris had asked me whether I knew the address of the studio in Amsterdam, and then promised he would try to fill in some of the gaps. Apparently something had already come of his efforts. We compromised: he would come around at one and see what the situation was by then. Another takeaway meal seemed likely.

The next two phone calls were business; I answered a question and dealt with an order. When the third one came, I picked up the receiver myself on the assumption that it would be more of the same, but a familiar voice spoke.

'Miss Hoare? Alan Quinn here. Do you have a minute?'

I rolled my eyes and turned my back on the buzz of conversation that was going on out front. 'Yes – hello, I'm just – can I help?'

'Ishmael Peters: have you seen him lately?'

I took a deep breath. 'Yesterday. Why?'

'We wanted to talk to him again, so I contacted the Amsterdam police and was told that he seems to have gone away. When I came in this morning I found a note saying he'd phoned here of his own accord yesterday evening. Do you know where he is?'

I told him where Peters had been yesterday, but warned him that he might not be there now.

He said, 'I'll call you back in a minute.'

When he did, he said simply, 'Checked out.' Was it my imagination, or did he sound fed up?

I was trying to remember. 'He said he was going back to Amsterdam today. Listen, there's something that I should probably tell you, something he was talking to me about. I don't know whether it's true, because he seems to be an habitual liar, but it has a bearing on Gabriel Steen's murder, if it is.'

I explained about Peters's claim that the fire had been set deliberately by someone who was looking for the manuscript I'd told him about, and about Peters's attempt to persuade me to part with it for my own safety's sake.

He responded with a deep silence and I added nervously, 'I don't see that someone who was looking for a valuable book would set fire to the place where they thought it might be hidden.'

'But it could have been an attempt to pressure him? Send him a message? Did you think that was what he was trying to tell you?'

'Yes. Maybe. He tried to say that they might find out about me and do the same here if I refused to hand it over to him. He tried to explain that he was just trying to save me trouble.'

'Has anybody been asking you about it?'

'I don't see how anybody could know I have it.'

The open line hummed for a moment. 'That is, unless either Steen or Peters told someone.'

'Actually, I don't have it here – it's locked up somewhere safe.'

'Good idea. What's your own security like?'

I didn't like what his question implied. 'I have it,' I said shortly. 'Monitored intruder alarm with a fire alarm and a panic button. I was thinking I'd be careful about keeping it set. But I can't believe his story. Would *you*?'

'I'd like to give him a chance to repeat it to me so I can find out.' Quinn's tone was acid. 'There is a real chance that all this is related to the murder, you know. In fact, I'd say it makes a lot more sense than thinking that some passing criminal took one look at Gabriel Steen on his bike and realized how much cash somebody like that would be carrying around. If you hear from Peters, tell him that I really do want to talk to him without any further delay. I'll get back to the Amsterdam police again. Keep in touch. And maybe . . . well, it can't hurt to keep your eyes open.'

I agreed and said goodbye. When I hung up, I found that I was breathless. I hoped he would phone back shortly to tell me that Peters had been found, and maybe arrested and locked up in the Chelmsford town jail. But that hadn't happened by the time I noticed Chris Kennedy's red head weaving between some customers and bobbing along the aisle in my direction. I was making business chat at the time with a collector who was interested in my clean first edition

74

of Conan Doyle's *The Sign of Four*. I passed him on seamlessly so that Barnabas could collect £225 for it, grabbed Chris's hand, drew him after me into the office, and pushed the door almost shut.

'We have to talk,' I whispered. 'I need your help.'

He growled, 'So I gather. Come on, grab Ben and we'll take off for half an hour. It's all right, Barnabas knows about it, he's been on to me.'

'You've been talking to Barnabas?' I hissed.

'Vice versa,' he corrected me. 'Come on!'

# Pure Grease

We climbed into the leather interior of the Jaguar, installed Ben on the tiny rear bench seat and took off, only to slide into the kerb at the northern end of the street. Chris switched off the engine and turned to me.

'What's going on?'

'What did Barnabas tell you?' We spoke at the same moment.

Chris chose to answer my question first. 'Your father phoned me at nine o'clock sharp to suggest that I should get down here and make myself useful. I'm paraphrasing. By the time I'd got out of bed and drunk two cups of coffee I decided he must be right, if only because it's so strange to find him asking me.'

'He didn't tell me he'd phoned you.'

'Dido, just tell me what's going on?'

What I told him was that I couldn't be sure whether Barnabas saw him as an emergency bodyguard, or another researcher in the cause.

'You're stalling,' he said perceptively. He was right.

I took a deep breath and started to bring him up to date on the fire in Amsterdam, Peters's arrival in London and his weird behaviour, and the threat – if there really was a threat. To round it off I confessed, 'I don't know how much of this to take seriously. But when I told Inspector Quinn, his reaction was that, although it was unlikely, I should take precautions. So I'm taking precautions, that's why both Barnabas and Ernie are going to be around all day today.'

'What about at night? The fire in Amsterdam was set at night.'

I went through my argument again: why would anybody

set fire to a place where they thought that something valuable, something they wanted to lay their hands on, was being kept? And on the other hand, I had a fairly serious security system that I certainly wasn't going to forget to set for the duration.

Chris was frowning through the windscreen. 'No argument with the second point. Promise? All right. I can't say anything about the first part, except that the police in Amsterdam know that it was arson.'

'It might not be connected?' I offered hopefully.

'The fire was started in Peters's premises. All right, maybe he'd cheated one of his customers out of a few euros. But wouldn't it be an unbelievable coincidence if it wasn't in any way related to all this? To Steen's murder?'

Ben said, 'I'm hungry.'

Chris said, 'Me too. Shall we get some hamburgers?'

Ben was enthusiastic, and I felt a sudden eagerness for all that grease, all those calories. 'With cheese,' I agreed. 'Where . . . ?'

'The chain place up beyond the roundabout does takeaway, and we might even get back to the shop inside the half hour if they aren't too busy there.'

So we parked illegally, as a lot of other people were doing, in front of the takeaway, and Chris and Ben went in to choose lunch. I slumped in the passenger seat, ready to smile sweetly at any parking attendant who turned up with his ticket pad, and spent five minutes doing a kind of mental juggling act. Why *would* you try to intimidate Ishmael Peters that way if it meant that you might destroy the big prize? But how could this possibly *not* be to do with Gabriel Steen's manuscript?

I looked up and saw the two of them emerging from the swing doors laden with two carriers. At the same time the problems magically reversed themselves in my mind. You would intimidate Peters by setting fire to his place either if you knew for sure that the thing you wanted wasn't there, or if there was something that you wished to destroy and the manuscript didn't come into the picture at all except as a red herring. It was still a little hard for me to believe that the mysterious book wasn't involved in this, but I could just about accept the scenario in which Peters had made a serious enemy somewhere and needed Gabriel's manuscript to fund his own escape. I had no more evidence for this than for any other possibility, but just for a second the idea made me feel better. The hamburgers dripping with hot fat and ketchup, and the sugar rush from the cola, both helped too. We were all a mess at the end of lunch, but Chris had hijacked a huge bundle of paper napkins from the restaurant, and we had cleaned ourselves up well enough to be able to drive off while the capped head of a traffic warden was still four or five cars to the south of us. Maybe today was going to be a good day after all.

'Back to the shop?'

'Not just yet,' I said. 'I think I know what Barnabas wanted from you, and he's probably right. I'd like to find out a lot more about Ishmael Peters. We don't even know for sure that he's telling the truth about his relationship with Gabriel Steen. Maybe it wasn't friendly at all. The police are focussing on Steen and what happened to him. Which is good. Do you have any way of finding out more about Peters himself?'

'Possibly. I don't have any contacts in the Amsterdam police force, though they might still be willing to help me because of the paper. But I do know one or two people who are working in the Netherlands for a news agency. I could ask them.'

'Good,' I said. 'Thank you. Chris . . . ?'

'Dido?'

I saw him cast an enquiring and amused glance in my direction.

'There's something else that might help, with luck. Carry on for a couple of streets. Turn left just after the next traffic light.'

'Should we drop Ben?'

'Having Ben there will help,' I said.

# Search

We pulled up at the kerb just in front of the Nayland
Hotel, facing the wrong way so that both Chris and
Ben were sitting on the pavement side of the car where they
would be clearly visible to anybody standing in the doorway
of the hotel.

Chris threw a sharp look at the sign. 'This was where
Peters was staying. But he's supposed to have left this
morning.'

I told him I knew that, but I had an idea, and it would
only take me a few minutes to check, but it had to be done
this minute. Then I avoided any further debate by springing
out, running around the car and up the stairs, and ringing
the bell.

The door, as I'd been praying, was opened by the same
girl. Katerina, her name tag reminded me. I could see from
something that flickered in her eyes that she remembered
me, too.

I pasted a friendly smile on my face. 'Katerina? Do you
remember me? I was here yesterday with my father –'
something about that picture made me stop, and I changed
the word – 'father-in-law. Mr Ishmael Peters?'

'Mr Peters gone away, has,' she informed me promptly.
Her accent was eastern European.

I said clearly, 'Mr Peters left something in his room. He
left a piece of paper and he needs it. He telephoned and
asked me to come and get it for him. Have you cleaned his
room yet?'

'I . . . go up now.' She threw a glance at the stairs. 'I call
Mrs Churchill?'

I smiled easily and said, 'Oh no, you don't have to do

79

that. I'm in a hurry. My little boy needs his afternoon sleep soon.' I pointed at the car and saw that Ben was watching me through the window. I blew him a kiss and turned back. I knew I had a soppy smile on my face. 'His name is Ben. Anyway, I have to hurry. Can you take me up to the room yourself? I will just need two minutes.'

She smiled across at Ben, looked at me, and hesitated. The hesitation disappeared abruptly. She must have noticed the five-pound note I had folded into my left hand. 'Come now,' she said.

She led the way up two flights of the wide staircase and along the passage to a room at the front of the building. We passed a wheeled cart containing cleaning equipment, fresh folded towels and sheets, and an assortment of small cakes of soap. The door of the room was standing open. She pushed it wide, smiled and gestured me in. I entered and found myself in what had once been a large front room with ornate cornices, but was now only half of the original space minus a cupboard-like bathroom in a corner. The walls were painted a kind of pinkish cream, which was matched by the linen on the twin beds, the rumpled chenille bedspreads, and two lamp shades. A small television sat on top of the chest of drawers. The rumpled bed linen and a bath towel were the only signs of habitation.

I ignored the voice inside me that was chanting, 'What a stupid idea, this isn't going to work, this is never going to work' and rushed to the bedside table to examine the contents of an ashtray and pull out the drawer.

Katerina said, 'I change.' Then she suited her actions to her words by tearing the sheets off the slept-in bed and dropping them in a bundle beside the door. Nothing flew out of the dirty sheets, and I found nothing in the drawer except a cheap plastic folder with the hotel's name on it, containing typed information sheets and a flyer for one of the local restaurants. I slammed the drawer and headed for the waste paper basket. That held an empty cigarette packet and the unopened back section of a local newspaper with yesterday's date. The drawers in the big chest were empty, with a smell of dust which would probably discourage you from unpacking your clothes into them.

I almost gave up at that point, but a twinge of stubbornness sent me into the bathroom, where I shut the door behind me and slid the lock shut. The bath mat lay damp on the floor in front of the tub. I lifted it and looked underneath, ran my fingers across the invisible top shelf in the medicine cabinet where I felt nothing except some kind of sticky residue, looked around wildly and saw the rubbish bin under the basin. There were a few oddments in it: a used toothpaste tube, a couple of wrappings from some chewing gum, and a scrunched-up sheet of pink paper which I flattened out. It was covered with printing – in Dutch. I didn't puzzle over it. I dropped it back into the waste paper basket, and it fluttered down, flipping over as it fell, so that I could see that there was writing on the back. And I had run out of time.

Katerina's voice outside the door was saying, 'Hello? Hello?'

I called, 'Just a second!'

I retrieved the paper and stuffed it into a pocket of my jeans, flushed the toilet and ran water in the basin to rinse my fingers. Then I picked up a dirty hand towel and was using it vigorously as I opened the bathroom door, shaking my head regretfully.

'It isn't here,' I told her. 'He must have left his receipt somewhere else. Never mind, I have to go now. Katerina, if you do find something, please leave it in the office here and I will phone and ask. And thank you very much.'

I held out the money and smiled, she returned the smile and took the note. I left her there and trotted down the stairs, out the front door, and into the car.

'What were you doing?' Chris asked impatiently. 'Somebody's getting a bit cranky, by the way.'

I turned to Ben, who was looking sulky. 'Nap time,' I said. 'Chris, I wanted to check whether Peters left anything there in his room, and I had to do it quickly. They hadn't cleaned the room yet, but it was a near miss. I suppose I should have known it would be a waste of time, but I keep thinking that it would be nice to know more about him. And the police don't seem to have any notion where he's gone. I had the idea that he was living in Gabriel Steen's flat, but they say he isn't there. Wait a minute, I did get something.'

What I had stuffed into the bottom of my pocket was a small flyer. The text was in Dutch, but I could make out that it was an advertisement for a bar in central Amsterdam. What I had noticed on the back was a series of large numerals scrawled with a blue ball-point pen. There was no mystery at all about them: I was looking at the shop's telephone number, complete with the 020 prefix that you have to use if you're phoning from outside Greater London. In the event, Peters had never bothered to phone me to ask about a book, make an appointment, or even just announce his arrival at the shop. He had always simply appeared there in George Street. So it seemed quite likely that I'd got the evidence to identify who had made those silent phone calls which had been bothering me. In the circumstances, the discovery made a lot of sense, though maybe not a nice lot. Still, I'd prefer to know the truth about Peters. It can be more dangerous when you are in the dark.

# Getting Good Advice

On Monday morning we woke up under a black sky. It wasn't raining yet, but it soon would be, and the air was still and damp, and tainted with the exhaust gases of the rush-hour traffic. While Ben was finishing his cereal, there came a great explosion overhead, one crack of thunder followed by a rush of hail. Mr Spock appeared hastily at the kitchen window, demanding instant shelter. I raised the window and slammed it down again as soon as my cat and a blast of icy air had entered. The weather was a good excuse to drive Ben to school, and that was handy because Barnabas and I had made two appointments for that morning, and I'd be needing the car.

I double-parked among the other mothers' cars outside the nursery school and kept an eye on Ben until he had vanished inside. Then I extricated my purple MPV, made a U-turn across the street, and headed back to the Essex Road with one eye on the dashboard clock. Traffic on the Highbury roundabout was solid and barely moving, as usual, but I bullied my way across. That roundabout is bad for my character. Barnabas's flat was only another nine or ten minutes' drive to the north, and I soon drew up outside his building and honked. The outer door opened smartly, and he marched down the steps to the path.

'I was waiting for you,' he said unnecessarily as he arrived and buckled his seat belt. 'We are due there in five minutes.'

'We won't be there by then,' I told him. 'But we'll get there not long after. He'll wait for us.'

'Do you have the note?'

'In my shoulder bag.'

I had scribbled a formal request for the object which was

83

being kept under lock and key to be released to my father, Prof B. Hoare. Leonard Stockton is a stickler for correctness, which is one of the things which you have to respect in a solicitor. I wasn't counting on finding a parking space outside his offices, so Barnabas would take it upstairs and I would be waiting for him on a double yellow line, engine running, ready for the getaway.

The last stage of our excursion involved a slow run in heavy traffic down to the British Library. Once again I held on at the gate, ignoring the enraged honking from the taxi drivers who objected to me blocking the bus lane, and watched Barnabas vanish through the library door. At that point I discovered I was so tense that my shoulders were aching. I wriggled them and stretched and headed toward Kings Cross and the road to the Angel.

When I got back to the shop, I scooped up the mail from in front of the letter slot and carried it into the office, where the red light on the answering machine was flashing away enthusiastically. Good: maybe business would be picking up at last. I set the mail to one side, picked up a notepad and pen, pressed the button, and discovered just how wrong I'd been.

First message: 'Ms Hoare, it's Laura Smiley. Will you phone me as soon as you get this, please? It's urgent. Thank you.' I was sure that I heard a kind of note in her voice which suggested it wouldn't be good news.

The second message was nothing. Silence. Another deliberately silent phone call? I stabbed at the button and deleted it.

The third message was a question about a book which I was pretty sure I had already sold. I wrote down the details.

The fourth and final message was another thirty seconds of silence, and yes, by this time I was sure that the silence *did* count as a message of some kind. For one thing, it was a long time for the caller to hold on and say nothing. Was it supposed to be frightening me? That was the last call. It was the first time that one of these things had been the final message, so I punched 1471 fast, before somebody else rang and spoiled it. The usual mechanical female voice told me, in tones that wandered meaninglessly up and down the scale, that the call was from a pay phone and that it had been made over an hour before. I couldn't really picture the mysterious heavy breather, let's call him Ishmael Peters for the sake of argument, still standing on some street corner waiting for me to ring him back; but I tried anyway and got no answer and then I turned to opening envelopes and trying not to waste time thinking about anything but business.

When the phone rang, I grabbed it and shouted, 'Hello!'

After a shocked hesitation, a voice said, 'Ms Hoare, it's Laura Smiley. Did you get my message?'

When I'd opened and closed my mouth a couple of times, I stammered, 'I . . . Sorry, I'm expecting an important phone call.'

'Well, I need to have a word with you. Will you be there for a while? I'll come straight over.'

I told her that I'd certainly stay here until she arrived, and tried to recover a little lost time by dealing with the phone call about the book. It only took me a couple of minutes, and by that time the detective sergeant's car was pulling up in front of the shop. I opened the door before she had to ring the bell, re-locked it, and ushered her into the office, where we settled in the chairs and exchanged cautious looks.

She said abruptly, 'What were you doing at the Nayland Hotel on Saturday?'

I almost denied the charge before I remembered. Honesty seemed the wisest policy. 'Looking for Ishmael Peters. I knew he was supposed to have checked out, but I wanted to catch him if he hadn't left yet.'

'Why?'

Maybe honesty wasn't the wisest policy after all. I said, 'That's not easy to explain.'

'Try me,' she commanded. 'I'd better say that Inspector Quinn has heard about a strange woman going into Peters's room, and he's asked us to try to find out who she was.'

I noticed in passing that I'd managed to incriminate myself unnecessarily. This is what happens when you have a bad conscience. 'I told you, it's complicated. Would it make sense for me to talk to Mr Quinn directly, since he's working on the murder investigation? Then he can ask any questions he wants cleared up. How did you know it was me?'

'The chambermaid described you. She said you were a nice young woman with a little boy driving a big beautiful Jaguar car, and that you were looking for your father, who was called Peters.'

'Father-in-law,' I corrected her automatically.

'Do you have DI Quinn's phone number?' she asked drily.

I shrugged, found his card stapled to the previous week's page of my desk diary, and tried his mobile. It rang twice and he answered, 'Quinn.'

I took a deep breath. 'It's Dido Hoare. DS Smiley, from Islington, is here. She says I should tell you that I called round to the Nayland Hotel on Saturday and had a look in Ishmael Peters's room. He'd already gone by the time I got there. Is there a problem?'

'Why did you do that?' His voice was stiff.

I was trying to imagine what I could possibly say to him that didn't sound a little insane. I compromised by telling him about Peters's visit to the shop and his attempt to persuade me to give him Gabriel Steen's manuscript on the grounds that it wasn't safe for me to keep. 'He claimed that the people who burned out his studio were looking for it, and that's why it wasn't safe.'

'That sounds far-fetched,' Quinn observed. Obviously he wasn't inclined to believe me. Neither was I, for that matter, but that's what Peters had said.

I took another deep breath and told him about the series of silent phone calls.

'Really? How many? When?'

I told him. I told him about finding the flyer with my phone number written on the back, and then I told him that the latest silent call had been made this morning, from a London pay phone. 'Which means,' I pointed out in case he had missed its significance, 'that it couldn't have been Peters himself unless he's still here in England?'

I waited. It seemed like a long time before I heard his voice again. 'We don't know where he is. He's dropped out of sight since Saturday morning.'

My heart jumped. 'You don't even know whether he's gone back to Amsterdam?'

'He was booked on a lunchtime flight on Saturday, but he didn't catch it. He might have gone back by train and ferry instead. The security is minimal for citizens of the EU travelling between EU countries, and it's pretty easy to get in and out without anybody paying much attention.'

'He has an American passport,' I reminded him sharply.

'And some Dutch residence documents, I believe.'

I said, 'Oh.'

'Anything else?' he asked, and I told him that there wasn't. 'Let DS Smiley have the note you found, if you would. We'll be in touch if there's anything else. Miss Hoare?'

I whispered, 'Yes?'

'I understand why you're curious about Mr Peters, in the circumstances, but I'd like to urge you strongly not to go searching through places where you don't belong.'

There wasn't much I could say, so I kept quiet.

'And I don't want to exaggerate, but stay awake. I noticed your security system: make sure you use it. Let me know if you have any trouble, anything at all, even if these silent calls go on. Please.'

I assured him that I would do all that and hung up. Then I scrabbled in the long drawer of the desk, found the crumpled pink flyer, and handed it over to Laura Smiley. 'He said to give you this.'

She nodded seriously. 'I was listening to what you told him, and I don't like it much. Be careful, right? Don't hesitate to phone us at the station if anything happens.'

I said, 'Right,' watched her slide the flyer into a little plastic pocket which she had been carrying in her shoulder bag, and saw her out.

# Nothing Happening

By Wednesday lunchtime nothing had happened, and it was driving me mad. When Ernie arrived he found the front of the shop deserted and me doing stretching exercises in the back room.

'Hey, Dido, am I late?'

'I don't know,' I lied. 'A bit, I guess. But there's nothing happening here anyway. Somebody came in a while ago and bought two books. I think I'm going to go and get something to eat now. Ernie . . .'

He flung his leather coat on to the hook and looked at me enquiringly.

'I'm going to issue an Easter catalogue.' We are still doing four catalogues a year. Some people are like Barnabas: they prefer to buy things from printed catalogues rather than electronic sites. It might be illogical, but people can feel that way about paper and print. 'Illustrated books. You can collect that section off our website, and I'll start adding and deleting when I come back downstairs.' It was more or less accidental that I added, 'When you've done that, will you look around the internet for anything on Gabriel Steen? If there's anything that mentions both him and Ishmael Peters, keep it.'

In fact, when I got upstairs and discovered that my lunch was going to consist of the last slice of stale bread, soaked in a mixture of milk and the only egg left in the fridge, fried with half a strip of bacon, and served with the last two pickled onions, I decided to give myself an hour to make a shopping list and buy food. As always, it took longer than I'd intended, and it was nearly four o'clock by the time I'd finished carrying the bags upstairs and into the kitchen. I went to check the answering machine in the sitting room, and discovered a new message from Barnabas warning me that he would be arriving before six o'clock. It sounded serious. I wondered what he had to tell me.

I was just erasing his message when the phone rang and I grabbed it, expecting to hear Barnabas's voice; but it was Ernie.

'Dido? Somebody's just come in. Can you come down?'

I asked cautiously, 'Customer? Is it anybody you know?'

I heard a cough and a short, 'No.'

In Ernie, this brevity was unusual; presumably the customer, if it was a customer and not an irate policeman or an old friend from Oxford, was standing within earshot. I could have used a cold drink, but I told him I'd be down as soon as I'd put the milk and yoghurt into the fridge.

When I pushed through the door of the shop I found that another little flurry of business was in progress. Ernie was just handing over one of our carrier bags to a short, scruffy-looking old man in glasses and a jacket with two buttons missing. I recognized a fellow member of the PBFA, a dealer who worked from home in Camden Town. He smiled and nodded. He didn't seem to be the person whom Ernie had called about. On the other hand, there was somebody lurking at the back of the shop near the travel books. I raised an eyebrow at Ernie, and he nodded and pointed.

'I'll be in the office,' he said. 'I found something funny.'

'I'll be there in a few minutes,' I told him, hoping that he meant funny-good, and walked around the end of the row of bookcases.

Ishmael Peters was standing with his back against the shelves on the rear wall and his eyes fixed on the spot where I had just appeared. He was silent.

I said, 'Hello. You're back already?'

He relaxed and shrugged. 'I didn't go. Changed my mind.'

I stared at him openly, trying to work out what he was doing here, and told him the truth: 'The police want to talk to you about something else, I think. They've been asking me whether I knew where you were. They said that you missed your flight on Saturday.'

89

He shrugged again. I was watching for some kind of emotion, some sign of worry or uncertainty or anger to cross his face, but he looked almost like a sleepwalker. I folded my arms, leant my shoulder against the corner of a book-case and waited.

He glanced to his right, to the open door of the office where the sound of faint humming and clicking was audible. 'Can we talk?'

'Absolutely,' I said.

We both waited for a while. One of us was going to out-stare and out-wait the other, and I had the advantage, because he was the one who had come looking for me. I smiled encouragingly.

'What about getting a drink?'

'I could make some coffee,' I agreed. 'Why don't you come into the office while I do that?'

He blinked. 'Isn't there a pub open around here?'

'Well,' I said, 'I could use a sandwich. Ernie? Are you all right if I go out for twenty minutes?'

'No problem.' Suddenly Ernie was standing in the doorway. He had popped into view so quickly that I got the idea he had been lurking just behind the door frame, ready for action.

The nearest pub, on the corner of Upper Street, was in its mid-afternoon slow period by the time we arrived: not empty, but quiet, with a choice of tables in the big L-shaped room. Ishmael looked around carefully, escorted me to a bench seat halfway between the bar and the toilets, and said, 'What'll you have?' A hunger pang reminded me that I still hadn't eaten lunch, so I asked him to get me a soft drink and a bag of crisps and kept my eyes fixed on him while he stood at the bar and ordered. There was some kind of discussion, and I saw him shake his head and gesture. I thought suddenly that he was looking tired and a little crumpled. After a moment he paid and returned with my sugar-and-caffeine jolt and what looked like a Scotch on the rocks for himself. He sat down beside me.

After a gulp of my drink and a mouthful of cheese-and-onion, I had decided where I was going. I said, 'I wasn't expecting to see you. So you didn't go back to Amsterdam.'

He shrugged. 'Nowhere to go. They won't let me into the studio, they say it's dangerous. Can't even get in to find out what the damage is, whether everything's really gone. The apartment's rented in Gabe's name, and they've got that sealed up too. I couldn't think what to do, so I turned around and came back.'

'Stopping at the Nayland again?' I asked sneakily.

'No.'

I waited, but that seemed to be it. I sipped at my drink and almost asked him how he was doing for money, but that would only invite another suggestion that I should give him lots.

'About the police trying to contact you,' I started casually.

He flashed me a glance. 'Give me a break! I'm fed up talking to policemen. Why don't they just find the assholes who killed Gabe and burned out my place, instead of bothering me? I can't tell them anything about what's happened.'

I smiled at him sweetly and said, 'Oh, I'm sure you could.'

I heard that odd, strained giggle again. It sounded more forced today. He took a deep breath and said, 'What are you saying?'

'For example, these phone calls you've been making to me over the past week. Silent calls, heavy breathing.'

He turned bright red. 'Not me. Listen, I stopped doing that when you told me.'

I drained my glass and sighed. 'I think I'd better get back to work. Unless there's really something you wanted to say?'

'Sorry, I was just wondering what's happening with the manuscript.'

'Nothing yet. It's gone for analysis. Instead of playing the fool, why don't you tell me how I can contact you when I do find out about it? My researcher is on the case, and there could be something within a few days.' I hoped so, anyway. I was starting to be as anxious as Ishmael to get this over with. 'And if you want to speed things up, you can send me some evidence that it's any of your business. A letter from the solicitor who's handling Mr Steen's estate, for example. Something that would stand up in court. You *know* the deal

91

Gabriel and I made, I don't see why I have to go on reminding you.'

My voice had risen, and I saw him throw a quick glance around the room. As though anybody there was interested. In case somebody was, I looked around too, but nobody was paying any attention to us.

I lowered my voice anyway. 'Just let me know where to contact you.'

'Sure thing. Look, I'm moving around, so I got a new cell phone – it's tri-band, you can get me anywhere in the world.' He pulled a pencil out of his breast pocket, picked up a beer mat, wrote a line of numbers on the back of it, and pushed it across the table. I checked it and slid it into my pocket. It was a bit beer-stained and ready to be replaced anyway.

He was pulling himself to his feet. 'Thanks. I'll go talk to the lawyer as soon as I get back there.'

'When are you leaving?'

'Depends.' He didn't say on what, he just grimaced and nodded at me and left the pub. I sat at the table for another minute, but I still couldn't see that anybody was showing any interest in his slightly abrupt departure, and certainly nobody followed him out. So I did. By the time I'd reached the street he had gone.

I was back at the shop before I began to debate whether I was going to phone Laura Smiley and tell her that he had called round, but I couldn't believe it would make any difference whether I did. It wasn't as though he had actually said anything worth hearing. They already knew that Peters was still in London. And if I did tell them and they tried the phone number, he would realize that I'd gone running to them about him at the first possible moment. Maybe he'd take offence and refuse to speak to me again, I wished. But a part of me decided I might find out that I actually *needed* to talk to him again. It was the part that won the argument, but it was a close call.

# Compelling

When I got back to George Street the shop seemed to be empty again, but the lights were on. I pushed the door open, shut it snappily behind myself, and called, 'Ernie, what did you mean about finding something funny? And look, I have to go and get Ben in a few minutes.'

But it was my father who appeared abruptly in the office doorway.

'Dido? What's going on here? Ernie says that you went off somewhere with Ishmael Peters. Wasn't that a little reckless?'

*Reckless?* 'Just down to the pub,' I said indignantly and quickly changed the subject. 'Barnabas, I haven't had anything to eat since breakfast. Do you want to come upstairs for five minutes while I grab a sandwich?' Ernie stood up at the desk and looked at me. Before he could open his mouth, I said to him, 'Are you all right until six o'clock? If you are, I'll come down then and lock up.'

He took the hint and nodded silently. Barnabas compressed his lips and also nodded, and I led the way up to the flat. First I went into the sitting room to check the answering machine. Nothing. Then I followed Barnabas into the kitchen and found him switching on the kettle and eyeing the tea bags.

'What about you?' I asked, getting in first. 'Any luck?'

'Don't change the subject. What did Peters want? I thought he was supposed to have gone back to Amsterdam.'

'According to him, he doesn't have a home there any more. The building where he had his studio is in a dangerous condition and Gabriel Steen's flat has been locked up by the police. I wonder whether he has any right to stay there

93

anyway? There's only his word for it. He said that when he realized he didn't have anywhere to go, he didn't catch his flight. He's staying somewhere in London.'

Barnabas raised both eyebrows with scepticism and reached for the kettle, which had boiled and switched itself off. Not being in the mood for his cool tea, I beat him to it, threw the switch again, and set about making a proper pot. While it was brewing, I slapped two slices of ham down on a slice of fresh bread, smeared on some mustard, turned it into a sandwich, and took a bite without bothering to cut it into ladylike pieces. When my mouth was free enough to speak, I waved the remains of the sandwich in the air and asked, 'Would you like one?'

'Tea,' my father commanded. I complied, and sat down at the table with him to finish my late lunch.

'Where is he staying, then?'

'He wouldn't tell me.'

Barnabas took a sip of his tea and poured in a little more milk to cool it down. 'That just makes me wonder all the more. A suspicious character. The police want to speak to him? Have you told them that you saw him today?'

'Not yet,' I mumbled around another mouthful of ham. 'No time. Got his mobile phone number. I have a problem. If I give it to them, he'll know that I did. He could just disappear.'

'Why would he do that?'

'Mmmn. Why is he doing anything?' I swallowed, then tried to explain. 'I can't work out what he's up to, but I think he must be trying to avoid the police. Maybe he just doesn't trust policemen?'

'Considering what little that we know of his story,' Barnabas said judiciously, 'that could be so. Old habits. And yet . . .' Obviously Barnabas was thinking about 1970, Vietnam and all that.

'Anyway, I didn't think there was much of a hurry, because I don't see how you'd trace the owner of a mobile phone unless it has a service contract of some kind. You can just go into a shop and buy one for cash, and then you top it up when you need to with a card you can buy at any

94

supermarket checkout. So I *could* phone Alan Quinn first thing in the morning and explain, but I don't see how he can do anything about it unless he has some way of persuading Peters to meet him.'

Barnabas said, 'A policeman might know what to do, whereas I believe that you don't. Now then, about the codex.' I waited. 'Dr Fletcher and I had a meeting this afternoon: that's the man at the Library, Terence Fletcher. He will be looking at the vellum and the inks as well as the nature of the text. So far, between us, we have listed the subject matter of the different sections: botanical, astronomical, biological, pharmaceutical. There are illustrations on most of the pages, which is helpful in one sense though rather confusing in another.' He looked at me significantly. When I refused to bite, he continued. 'It must have struck you that the drawings are of unidentifiable things? No? I assure you, the plants, for example, seem to be entirely unknown to science. Some of the astronomical figures are familiar, in mediaeval terms, but others are not. In sum, the illustrations – which appear on all but a couple of dozen pages, incidentally – are rather crude and unrealistic in modern terms, but very vigorously done. "Compelling" is the word Fletcher used. The text, of course, is just as fascinating as the pictures and so far just as unreadable, or even more so.'

I said, 'What does all that add up to?'

'It's inconclusive.'

I groaned. 'How? What are you saying?'

'I'm starting to wonder whether the nature of the whole thing might remain a mystery – though Fletcher has managed to garner a little negative evidence. The vellum is genuine, and it is old. The inks are types which are not now manufactured, or at least not commercially, though you could probably make your own if you wanted to: Fletcher had several suggestions for recipes. He has arranged for a spectroscopic analysis of the most common one. The pictures are touched up with watercolour washes. The text has been written, or perhaps it might be more accurate to say "drawn", with a quill pen, not a . . . a Parker fountain pen, as it were, using a strong brown ink; but various other colours and shades of ink also appear from time to time. The text as you must have noticed resembles late mediaeval handwriting, possibly in a Florentine style, Fletcher suggests, but using an unfamiliar alphabet. None of this is evidence of the source or authorship of the manuscript, it merely tells us a few things that it is not. There might be something in the text which would tell us more, if only we could read it.'

'You can't read anything?'

'Not a word.' He sounded surprisingly cheerful, given what he was saying, and I could see that he was enjoying the hunt. Maybe that was the point of it all for a scholar. For me, though, it wasn't. I have a decent degree from Oxford University, but I would never have made a good academic, I don't have the patience. I don't enjoy just scraping away at the edges of big, big mysteries. I need answers.

I said, 'I'd better go and get Ben. Can you wait here?'

By way of reply, he poured himself another cup of tea.

# Wading Through Glue

B y the time I'd finished the nursery school walk next morning, I had come to a decision. It was a dry, dark day with a bitter wind from the east, and I was trotting back to try to keep warm. I got as far as the toy shop at the end of the street and then skidded to a stop without even knowing what I intended to do. Apparently I was going to take a precautionary look around the corner in case I ran into an ambush. But as far as I could see, Ishmael Peters was not lurking anywhere there, so I crossed the road soberly and went straight to the door of the shop and in.

It was only just after nine, almost an hour before we were due to open up. I locked the door again, turned off the alarm, and continued into the office without turning on the lights in the shop. Inside the back room, the little windows high up in the rear wall did nothing to relieve the day's gloom; I switched on the desk lamp, pushed the door to, and turned on the computer. I had a phone call to make, but I wanted to think a little bit about how to handle it. There was one message showing on the answering machine. Hoping against hope that it was something I actually wanted to hear, I pressed the button and listened to a couple of second's silence. Then the too-familiar voice.

'Uh, Miss Hoare? Just calling to say hi, hope you're OK.' Click. Presumably he was going to be leaning over my shoulder like this until one of us died of old age, or at least until I managed to get rid of the manuscript. I wondered whether – if he got too pushy and I got too bored with him – I shouldn't just send the thing to one of the big auction houses after all, with a very small reserve on it. I calculated that if it only sold for £3,500, I'd almost break even. Even if it made less than that, at least I'd be able to spend my time doing other things. It might actually be worth it.

I couldn't put off making the call much longer. I reached for the phone and then remembered something else and looked at the computer screen. Yesterday, Ernie had been saying that he'd found something 'funny'. In the toing and froing that had followed, I'd forgotten to ask him about it. But there was a new internet file saved on the screen under the name 'Dido'. I opened it, and at first I wasn't sure of its relevance. But when I settled down to read it through, I found that it was a five-year-old news item about the smuggling of antiquities from Italy to the USA. A former Getty Museum curator and an unnamed art dealer based in Paris had been accused of 'illegally obtaining' twenty-six items during the 1990s and selling them through auction houses in London and New York. The name of the jailed ex-curator was Henry Roane, Jr. No name was given for the 'old art dealer', but one prosecution witness in the case was identified as 'Ishmael Peters'.

I read through the piece twice and then made a second copy for safety's sake and shifted the files into a couple of folders where they would at least be out of sight. Then I looked carefully at the screen to make sure that this was the only thing Ernie had left for me. He was taking classes today, not due to come in. I tried his mobile and left a message for him to phone me when he had a spare moment. 'How?' and 'What else can you find out about Peters?' not to mention, 'Ernie, what's the earliest you can get here in the morning?' were questions that would have to wait until he was free to talk.

I called the police station next, asked for Laura Smiley, and absent-mindedly interrupted her greetings with, 'I need advice.'

She said politely, 'Go ahead.'

I told her the story and wound up with, 'And I have no idea where Peters is staying. "Not at the Nayland," is what he told me, and I suppose that's true since it would be so easy to check. The only thing I have is a mobile phone number for him. I'm supposed to contact him there if there's any news about this manuscript that Gabriel Steen left with me. The thing is, if you people try to phone him he'll know that I've been talking to you, and that might make things even more difficult.'

I listened to a silence which continued for so long that in the end I broke it with, 'Hello?'

'I'm thinking. Would that really matter? And you aren't quite right about the phone. If we had good reason, we could get a 522 order requiring the network operator to inform us which cells the phone has been using. We could locate him to within a few hundred yards if we really had to. Not everybody knows about this, and there's no reason why he should, which is probably why he bought that phone, yes. But why would he care? On the other hand, if he's worrying you, it might not hurt to tell him that we're in touch. Would you say he's harassing you? Or trying to? If he is, it might not be a bad idea to let him know you've told us about him.'

It was so sensible that I was almost reassured.

'I won't try to make up your mind for you, but if it was me, I'd give Quinn an update. He'll appreciate having it confirmed that our man is still in London, and Peters might have said something to you that Quinn would find helpful.

'And if you want to keep in Peters's good books at the same time, I can even suggest something about that. What about phoning his number yourself, as soon as you've spoken to Quinn, and telling Peters that Quinn would like him to contact them? Maybe he wouldn't mind doing that, I have no idea, but at least he won't have any reason to think that you aren't being honest with him. He couldn't expect you to keep quiet if Quinn actually asked you about him, if you see what I mean. Could he?'

I agreed that he couldn't, though a sliver of doubt remained in my mind. It was still no easier for me to guess what Peters was really up to.

In the end, I let her sneaky arguments persuade me. Nothing would make Ishmael Peters disappear from my life as long as I was his only link to Gabriel's manuscript, so it couldn't matter much whether he was fed up with me. We would just have to put up with the mutual annoyance.

I dug Alan Quinn's card out of my wallet and rang his mobile. Unlike Ernie, he answered at once.

I gave my name.

'Miss Hoare. Everything all right?'

Was it my imagination, or was his voice cooler than it had been a few days ago? I told him I had some news. 'Ishmael Peters came by the shop. He is in London. He didn't say where he's staying, but he seemed to be suggesting that he'd be here for a while.'

'He didn't say why?'

'He told me that he'd changed his mind about going back because he can't get into his studio and the police have sealed up Gabriel Steen's flat, which is where he was living.'

'I think I'd take anything Mr Peters told you with a pinch of salt. Steen's flat is not a crime scene, and it has not been "sealed up" by anybody. Peters can get into it if he has the right to – or, at least, the keys.'

There was something going on. I waited for him to say more.

'He didn't hint where he's staying while he's here?'

'No. I assume it's because of Gabriel Steen's manuscript. He just gave me the number of his mobile phone so I could get hold if him if – if I have to, that's all.'

'Why don't you let me have that? I'll pass it on to some people who want to contact him.'

I had recited the number before I thought about what he had just said. '*Who* wants to contact him? Not you?'

'He's not a suspect in Gabriel Steen's murder. That's all that interests us.'

'He's not?'

'We've been able to confirm that he wasn't in this country when Steen was killed. So far as I'm concerned, that's all that matters until something new comes up.'

I thought about what he was saying to me and asked, 'What's happened? You were interested in Peters when I last spoke to you. He's the one who has Steen's copy of the agreement we signed. You have to be interested in what he's up to.' I wasn't going to mention the silent telephone calls, but they were a good enough reason to be sure that Peters was up to *something*.

'That's true to some extent, but even if he were next-of-kin, that doesn't mean he needs to be investigated by us.'

There was something that wasn't being said. I gave a mental shrug and said, 'All right then. I told DS Smiley about the mobile phone number, and she's the one who suggested I should contact you. Never mind.'

'Thanks anyway,' he said, almost without hesitation. 'I'll pass it on.'

This was starting to be the kind of wading-through-glue conversation I'm used to having with police detectives. I tried one last time. 'Pass it on to . . . ?'

'The Dutch police want to talk to him about the fire. And there are some people based at New Scotland Yard who deal with art problems. They've been interested in Mr Peters for a few years.'

If it hadn't been for Ernie's detective work on the internet, I would have been at a real loss here. As it was . . .

'Oh yes,' I said airily. 'You mean SO1, Art and Antiquities. The last thing I heard, there were only about four of them working there and everybody was saying they're too stretched to be able to do much.'

'They're very persistent,' he said solemnly. I could have sworn he was trying not to laugh.

We said a more friendly goodbye after that, and I hung up and stared for a while at the computer screen. By now, it was showing a restful screen saver, a picture of trees in a forest. I went on watching the landscape fade and re-form for a while. Then I stuck my 'back-in-five-minutes' sign on the door and went upstairs to wash my face and try to wake up enough to think things through. After half an hour, I'd decided to stick to the plan that Laura Smiley had suggested. I almost made the mistake of calling Peters from my unlisted home telephone, but I caught myself just in time and went back down to the shop where he already knew the number. Then I discovered that his mobile was also switched off. Never mind: the post had arrived by the time I'd got downstairs, which gave me a chance to mind my own business for half an hour. But while I was pretending to read a catalogue, I was really thinking about other things. Eventually it occurred to me that I wasn't taking anything in and might as well leave this chore to Barnabas. Or even Mr Spock, for all the good I was doing.

They say that when your mind is empty new ideas pop up from nowhere. No sooner had I realized that my mind was as blank as a fresh snowdrift, than something did pop in. Not an answer, but another question: why was Gabriel Steen carrying the manuscript with him when he rode up to sell me some ordinary Victoriana?

On Thursdays, I am supposed to sit in the shop all day and mind it like a responsible businesswoman. I opened the file that Ernie had left for me again and copied the link on to the back of one of my business cards. Then I paused long enough to find a black marker in the drawer of the desk, whisk a sheet of paper out of the printer, and prepare a neat sign which said that I was very, very sorry, and wished to apologize to my many disappointed customers, but the shop would be closed for a few hours this morning while I was out on urgent business. I stuck it to the glass of the door with some tape, set the alarm, locked up, and went to look for a taxi.

# Magic Pictures

The cab dropped me in Euston Road, just short of the gates to the British Library. I trotted across the forecourt, pushed my way through the glass doors, looked for the reception desk, side-stepped a group of three middle-aged men who were intent on getting to the coffee shop, told the woman at the desk that I wanted to see Dr Terence Fletcher, and gave her my name. I waited for her to ask me whether I had an appointment, but instead she spoke to somebody on her internal phone, nodded, and asked me to wait.

I barely had the time to finish reading the notice about opening hours and day passes, when I saw him striding through the crowds with his eyes fixed on me: a man in his early forties, with a smooth, bony face and tidily brushed brown hair, wearing neat jeans and a dark blue jacket.

He braked to a halt. 'Miss Hoare? Professor Hoare didn't tell me that you were coming here today.'

'My father didn't know,' I admitted. 'I'm supposed to be at the shop, but I suddenly started to wonder about some more things, and I thought I'd take the chance that you'd be here. I hope I'm not interrupting your work if I ask you a few questions?'

'You're the person who owns the manuscript, I gather. No, you're very welcome; I'm not doing anything I can't put off. Will you come up to my office?'

We climbed a wide staircase to the floor above, turned right and followed a long corridor to an open door with his name on it, and entered a small space containing a desk with a computer and a drift of papers, three chairs, and some crowded bookcases. There was also an electric coffee maker on a side table.

He gestured. 'I can fix some coffee in a minute if you'd like that. Oh, and I have your photographs in a file here, but if you want to look at the codex, I'll have to go and get it. It's locked in one of our secure rooms. If you'd like to wait a minute . . .'

I told him that the photographs would probably be all we needed and that I'd had enough coffee already this morning. He waved me to a seat, sat on the edge of his desk chair, propped his elbows on the desk, stared at me and said, 'You know, this thing your father brought is the strangest manuscript I've ever handled. I don't have any easy answers for you, not yet.'

I assured him that I hadn't expected any, and that Barnabas had brought me pretty well up to date. Then I jumped to the point.

'Do you often get to see things like this with no provenance and no way of reading it? I don't mean you, personally, I mean the curators of public collections.'

He pursed his lips, hesitated, and said, 'No. In a word. Of course things keep turning up, it would be silly to say that they don't. Sometimes they're offered to us directly by organizations that need the money, often to restore old buildings, things like that. And like most museums, we buy interesting items from the auction houses or specialist dealers. We just bought a very nice fourteenth-century illuminated manuscript from Quaritch – I'm sure you know them.'

I don't operate on their level, but I certainly do know Quaritch. Everybody does. They issue the kind of catalogues that make you gasp in admiration, even though you can't afford to buy anything.

I said, 'It's old. It could have been gathering dust in something like a church collection, a monastery library, something like that? If nobody can read it, then it might just have been forgotten?'

He was still hesitating. Eventually he said, 'That's possible, though I would have said that most of the old stuff of European origins has largely been rooted out of those places in the last sixty years. A lot of stuff came to light after World War Two. We do have some things in the collection here that resemble your manuscript in many ways. I'll show you on your way out, if you like.'

'But you can read those?'

He nodded.

'Barnabas told me you can't read this one.'

'I *can't* read it, not really, but I can *read* the illustrations, in one sense. They're like some in our collection here. We have one book that was published in France in 1620 with similar kinds of pictures – something called the *Ars Notoria*.'

I told him Barnabas had mentioned it.

'And there are the Sloane manuscripts, too. What I'm trying to say is that there are lots of things I could show you that have illustrations similar to yours. Generally they're about necromancy, the forbidden arts, and they were kept hidden for a long time by the ecclesiastical authorities and also by private collectors who didn't want to get into trouble for keeping something about the black arts.'

'Barnabas told me that. He did say that the subject matter of some of those pictures is like what's in our manuscript.'

Fletcher nodded. 'Very similar. I could point you to a lot of . . . Look, can I show you something?'

When I said that he could, he led the way out of the room and sped off toward the stairs, with me trotting after him. This time we were going down. We doubled through the lobby, took a narrower flight to the floor below, went through a pair of swing doors under a sign which said 'Staff Only', and halfway down a brightly lit, deserted passageway to a door with a security light flashing above it and a complicated control panel in the wall beside it. He placed himself between me and the panel so that I couldn't see what he was doing, punched some buttons, stuck a fingertip against a small screen, and undid two locks. As the door opened, the lights came on inside.

'You see,' he assured me, 'this strong room is absolutely secure. Fireproof, too.'

We were standing in a small room, maybe five or six metres square, filled with rows of tall wooden cabinets containing drawers. There were no windows in the room, and it felt airless despite the soft breath of air conditioning.

He stopped, considered, and then went to a shallow drawer labelled MS 17123 and slid it open. The contents were hidden by a covering sheet of thick white cloth. He slid the drawer out fully, pushed the cover back, and put on a pair of pristine white cotton gloves from a box sitting on top of the cabinet. He beckoned, and I joined him and found him carefully opening a red leather binding and revealing a picture of two demons, complete with horns, hoofs and tails, shrinking away from a masterful-looking person in a blue robe who was shaking a finger at them. He looked like a headmaster dealing with a couple of naughty schoolboys, and it was obvious that the demons were in serious trouble. On the verso was a diagram drawn with a quill pen in the familiar shade of brown ink; it contained a circle divided by seven straight lines radiating from the centre, with rows of writing circling around the central point.

'This is a magic circle for summoning spirits of air,' Fletcher said in a hushed voice.

'It is a bit like some of the diagrams in our manuscript,' I agreed.

'But there is a difference. Can you read this text?'

'A few words,' I admitted. 'Well, "*Meridies in qua dominent . . . an . . . angeli*". I can make out a title, with the help of a dictionary, but I've forgotten most of my Latin.'

'I can read it,' he said. 'I can manage most of the manuscripts in here. My speciality. But I can't read yours. Sometimes I think that I've made out a phrase, but by the next day I've decided that I was mistaken, I'd simply misinterpreted what I was seeing. By the way, would you like to look at yours now? It's locked up in one of these drawers.'

'Don't bother,' I said. 'I take your point. It's certainly safe here, whatever it is. You won't let anybody but me take it away, will you? That includes my father. I don't suppose he'll want to, but you never can tell, if he gets a bright idea. I'm not sure it's safe. Did Barnabas tell you that the last man who was carrying it around was murdered?'

Fletcher stared at me. 'What? When?'

Oh. So Barnabas had been discreet. I told him that there

might not have been a connection, but Terence Fletcher was nobody's fool. He gently replaced the volume, slid the glass back into place and shut the drawer. Then he tossed the gloves back into the box, and we headed toward the door and the outside world. The business of locking the room was as complicated as unlocking it had been. Yes, Gabriel Steen's manuscript was safe from anything other than a very large bomb. Or a court order.

I watched him pull himself together, and decided not to go any further down that path.

'So, you see, your drawings are similar, though I'd say not as good as the best of the ones that we have here. They're very lively, but we're not looking at a first-class illuminated manuscript, for example. Though it is probably older than what I've just shown you, and perhaps that's why it seems cruder.'

It left one big question. 'Could the whole thing be a fake? A kind of copy? For example, could *you* make something like mine?'

He stared at me. 'What do you mean?'

I said, 'You're an expert. You know all about this kind of thing. Would it be possible . . . practical . . . for you to make an artefact like it and try to sell it? Are we looking at a hoax?'

He stared at something on the wall over my head. 'I don't think I could. No, not really. Mind you, people have done it. It's a very specialist skill, and don't think I could. You'd have to find blank vellum old enough to match the penmanship. Even with an unknown script, it would take months of work for an expert. It's a very labour-intensive thing.'

I wasn't quite convinced, so I tried another tack. 'If you did try, and you managed to produce something like our manuscript, how would you go about selling it, and how much money would you expect to get?'

He laughed suddenly. 'I wouldn't try to sell it because I'd be afraid of getting caught. If it was a genuine find, I'd . . . I'm not sure. There was a time, a few years back, when a lot of art was being sold surreptitiously to rich Americans. I suppose I'd think of selling in New York too. I don't know how I'd do it, though, because there are regulations nowadays about exporting manuscripts. You must know about them.'

I agreed that I did. I even owned a copy of a notice which the Department of National Heritage had issued a few years back. I couldn't remember the details now, but I knew it was on a shelf in the office and I could remember that it outlined detailed and incredibly difficult conditions which would make the export of something like Steen's manuscript very restricted, maybe illegal. I'd better have a look for it when I got back and find out whether the regulations meant that Gabriel had smuggled it out of the Netherlands, in which case . . . What would that mean?

'There's one other thing,' I said quickly. 'Would you look up this address on the internet? It's something about an old forgery case. One of the people who was involved with that is connected with our codex: he claims that he was the partner of the man who brought it to me, and that he owns a share in it. I was wondering whether it gives you any ideas about the codex.' I handed him the internet address which Ernie had found.

He frowned down at what I had given him. 'You know the way out? Yes. I'll do that of course.'

# The Police are Here

I was back in George Street by twelve thirty. The shop looked exactly as it had when I'd left, and there were no queues of disappointed customers at the door. I could have gone inside and opened up for business: customers do often turn up at lunchtime. But somehow I'd lost interest. I swerved towards the side door, climbed the stairs, let myself into the flat, was greeted by Mr Spock, and went straight on into the bathroom to turn on the taps and fill the tub. All my clothes were smelly. I dumped everything into the laundry hamper, heated up the coffee that was left over from breakfast, and got back in time to keep the bath from overflowing. By one o'clock I was lying slumped in the warm water with my coffee mug in one hand. Despite the fact that my eyes were closed, I was aware of Mr Spock jumping on to the edge of the bath tub and settling there to supervise.

Bliss.

When I heard the phone ringing I just slid down lower. There was another phone call a while after that, but the water was too warm to abandon. I yawned and dozed and only woke up when I dropped my mug into the water. Mr Spock was still sitting there comfortably with his eyes shut.

In the end I was roused by the sound of the downstairs door slamming, hasty footsteps climbing the stairs and a key turning in the lock, followed by my father's bellow. 'Dido?'

Before he had time to join me in the bathroom, I called, 'What's wrong?'

He stopped just before he reached the open door. 'What are you doing?'

I told him I was in the bath and asked again whether something was wrong.

'Aside from your going missing, nothing in particular.'

We discussed the etiquette of my shutting up shop on a business day and vanishing without warning him of my intentions while I was drying off and wrapping myself in my terry bathrobe. Then as I dashed across the hall to the bedroom, I added, 'Besides, I went to see Dr Fletcher. He's interesting, isn't he?'

'Very dedicated,' my father agreed. 'Why did you?'

'I wanted to talk to him about the codex, partly because I want to be able to say something sensible to Ishmael Peters next time he gets in touch with me and partly because I really need to know what it is. What it's worth. I didn't really get much from him, except that it seems to be impossible to guess what it's worth. It's hard to know what to do with it.' I could have added that I was feeling a little inadequate to the task of deciding. And dealing with Ishmael Peters. Under-prepared, in fact.

'I'm going to make myself a ham sandwich. Do you want one?'

'Not really,' Barnabas admitted.

I explained that ham was all that I had, so we discussed the problem and agreed that a quick visit to the sandwich bar in Upper Street might be a good idea. On the way out, I stopped to listen to the messages on my answering machine. They were both from Barnabas. I deleted them as soon as I heard his voice and led the way downstairs and around the corner.

Back at the end of half an hour, we turned into George Street and found something new there. At first glance it seemed that a couple of customers had turned up at last. Two men, wearing buttoned-up suits under open coats, were hanging about in front of the shop. The one with blond hair was looking alternately at my hand-printed sign and his wristwatch, while the second was staring into space. There was also a parking warden, who seemed to have already ticketed a raft of illegally parked cars on the other side of the street. Funnily enough, as he crossed the road to walk up the near side and passed the blue saloon car which was parked on the double yellow lines near my door, I saw him look hard at something on the windscreen and walk on without pausing. One of the waiting men caught his eye and nodded, which told me all that I needed to know.

'The police are here,' Barnabas muttered. He had seen it too.

I automatically looked across to make sure that my own car was legally parked in one of the residents' bays, though I already knew that it was, and picked my way between the two visitors, keys in hand.

'Miss Dido Hoare?' one of the men asked.

I resisted the temptation to say no, I was the Duke of Edinburgh, and substituted, 'I'll be with you in a minute.' Then I went through the necessary procedures, turned off the security system, and watched Barnabas usher the two of them inside and wait for them to produce their identification. That formality over, we stood in the aisle and I said, 'Can I help you?'

'Miss Hoare, DI Quinn of the Essex force gave us your name in connection with a person we're trying to reach, a Mr Peters. I understand you're in touch with him?'

'He told me that Art and Antiquities was interested in Mr Peters,' I said thoughtfully, wishing I'd bothered to look properly at the names on their cards. 'That's you? What exactly is the problem?'

It didn't work, of course. 'We just want to have a word with him. We understand that he's in London?'

'Well,' I said slowly, 'on Monday he was, which is when I last saw him, and he did say he was staying for a while. He didn't tell me where, but he gave me his mobile number. Do you want that?'

'If you don't mind. Thank you, Miss Hoare.'

'Wait a minute.'

I left the detectives there under my father's watchful gaze and went into the office, where I grabbed a pad of paper, copied Peters's number off the beer mat which was now settled into the bottom drawer of the desk, and returned with pen and pad.

I ripped the top sheet off and gave it to the talkative one. 'That's it. If he gets in touch with me again, I'll tell him you want to speak to him. Will you write down your names and phone numbers here, please?'

I handed over the pad, and the silent detective printed two names, one phone number and an extension number and handed it back. I glanced at it. DI Colin Page, DS Michael Garner, and the telephone number for Scotland Yard. That seemed to finish their business with me. I saw them politely out the door and watched them get into their car, pause for a second, then drive off.

'What was that about?' Barnabas demanded. 'They could have saved a lot of time by phoning.'

I speculated that they had been in the neighbourhood, or maybe they had just wanted to see for themselves whether Ishmael Peters was camping on one of our bookshelves. There was no time to discuss it: I had noticed the light flashing on the answering machine when I'd gone into the office. There were several messages waiting.

The first was the one I wanted: Terence Fletcher, asking me to phone him. The second caller had hung up. The third was Pat – my older sister – and she was asking me to phone her urgently. Her voice didn't sound particularly urgent, just gossipy. She probably wanted to complain about something, and I could leave that until the evening. The last was Chris Kennedy saying he would try me again as soon as he was clear of meetings at the newspaper. That would probably be early evening, if they were not too busy there.

I called the number that Dr Fletcher had left and identified myself.

'Miss Hoare! Hello, sorry I missed you earlier. I did have a look at that report. You must have realized that it's just the kind of thing I was telling you about. In fact, I vaguely remember that case. There was a lot of publicity, and I think some people got prison sentences.'

I waited for him to make the obvious comment, but all he added was that the Getty case had been much discussed by library and museum staff while it was going on. 'Of course,' he finished, 'that was works of art, not manuscripts, but the same principles apply. Did you think that maybe the codex was intended to go the same way? Obviously I can't tell from what I know, but it's possible.'

I had been waiting for him to pick out the name of Ishmael Peters – but apparently it hadn't made enough of an impression to sound familiar to him, and so all I'd got was a kind of general assurance that I could go on looking in this direction, which did fit with the interest of the men from Scotland Yard in knowing Peters's whereabouts. I promised I'd get in touch with him if had any more questions, while he promised to get in touch with Barnabas if he made any discoveries. At least by now it was pretty clear that the codex was safe until I could get rid of it; but how to manage that was still a puzzle.

Barnabas was waiting. 'Well?'

'No news.' I summarized the argument in favour of some kind of smuggling scheme and pointed out that there could be legal problems.

Barnabas listened without comment until I'd finished. Then he merely said, 'It would explain what Gabriel Steen was doing with it in London, if it turns out that this was the first stage in the same kind of process.'

I had to agree, but I didn't much care for it. I had known Gabriel Steen for a long time, and I'd liked him. If you had asked me even ten days ago, I would have said without a second's hesitation that he was an honest man.

# Blow-up

I shmael Peters sat in my kitchen. He was backed into the corner behind the table, tied up to one of the chairs, snarling at me like an old wolf. I was angry. Outraged. Desperate.

I screamed, 'Tell me what it is!'

He started to swell with anger, straining against the ropes that lashed his hands to the back of the chair.

I looked around for inspiration. The kitchen scissors were lying on the draining board. I picked them up, opened the blades, and took two small steps toward him, hissing. He was going to tell me where the damned thing had come from, what it was, what it meant, or I was going to cut off his ponytail. He watched me. He was swelling up like a balloon, twisting against the ropes that held him there.

'Tell me *now*!'

But he couldn't or wouldn't. He twisted in the chair and went on swelling until his body exploded into a million pieces and vanished.

I opened my eyes. The flat was quiet, and the sky was dark outside the bedroom window. I didn't bother to look at the clock because it was still quiet outside, no traffic sounds. The bell in the tower of the big church a little to the south struck twice. It sounded much nearer in this silence. So I had a little more time to sleep, if I could. And I hadn't actually needed to be warned that my thoughts were becoming unpleasantly fixated on Ishmael Peters and the codex. The dream, though, had left me wondering whether this wasn't bad for my character.

It struck me that the dream was late in coming, because during the evening I had recruited some help that I could trust: Chris Kennedy. Barnabas had politely absented himself,

114

and being without a babysitter, Chris and I had phoned out for a Chinese takeaway and eaten it at the kitchen table, with lashings of soy sauce and hoi sin, lots of paper napkins, and a complimentary bottle of pink wine. And I told him the full version of the story of Gabriel Steen and his mysterious parcel, our agreement, his murder – and now Ishmael Peters. Some time at the beginning of the tale he had asked me for some paper, produced a large black pen from his breast pocket, and started taking notes. I'd been in the hands of a professional interviewer, and I'd discovered that I was able to tell him more than I'd told anybody else.

By eleven o'clock, even a pot of fresh coffee was failing to keep me awake, and he had got to his feet, looked for a moment at the stack of notes as he bundled them together, kissed me on the tip of my nose, and said, 'Dido, I'll do everything that I can. I'll go back to my contact in Amsterdam and ask him whether he can find anything more about Steen and Peters. I have an obvious explanation if he asks: I'm putting together a special piece on Gabriel Steen, you understand? Human interest with a touch of whodunnit. I might even write it, if things work out. Stop worrying. All right, that was a silly thing to say. You know what I mean. I love you.'

I remembered saying, 'I love you too, and I'll try,' and seeing him to the door of the flat. We were just outside the door of the bedroom, where Ben was sleeping so that it was no place to risk a long conversation, but he turned on the landing and muttered, 'There's one thing. You were asking this man at the British Library about the report of the smuggling business? The Getty case? I'll have a look at that tomorrow. And something occurs to me right now: if Ishmael Peters acted as a witness for the prosecution, that doesn't mean he was on the side of the law, it just means that he knew about the smuggling scheme. He could have done a deal with the prosecution, you know. It happens all the time. It would just mean that they were more interested in getting a judgement against the other defendants. The bigger fish. I believe that happens even more in the US than here. I'll find out about it.'

I went to bed feeling easier, and eventually fell asleep.

# Turning on the Lights

I let myself into the shop, turned the lights on, patrolled the aisles while I tidied up one or two shelves that needed attention, and marched into the office. Ernie wasn't due until lunchtime. Barnabas had phoned nearly an hour before to assure me that he was feeling well and would arrive at any minute. I remembered something and pulled the visitors' chair over to the filing cabinet, climbed on to it so that I could reach the shelf with its collection of old catalogues, out-of-date auction records and oddments, and found what I was looking for: the Department of National Heritage guidelines on export licenses; a plastic-bound forty-page computer printout of the rules. I clambered down with it, flapped the dust off, and opened it at the desk. It was detailed and fascinating. I hadn't known before that you will need a license if you wish to export wallpaper more than fifty years old which is valued at over £39,600. The same rule applied to books. As for manuscripts and documents more than fifty years old, the rules were tougher: any sale for even the smallest price required a license.

It was time to get a grip on business matters. I could remember thinking exactly that on several occasions recently. I stowed the regulations in the top drawer of the filing cabinet in case I needed to consult them again. Then, feeling virtuous, I swept up a little heap of unopened mail from the packing table and set about sorting it before anything else could happen. I'd been able to throw most of it away, log three cheques and write out a deposit slip, and then look through the most promising of the new catalogues before I heard the key in the street door and knew that Barnabas had arrived at last.

I'd barely opened my mouth before he interrupted. 'Dido? I have a question. Why did Gabriel Steen have the manuscript with him that day? Did he bring it to offer it to you?'

I was sure it hadn't been planned, and repeated the story of the phone call.

'You're sure? Then I can only repeat: why did he have such a valuable item in his pocket?'

'Actually, it was in his rucksack with his dirty underwear. But he didn't say.' As soon as I finished my smart-aleck reply I regretted it, because the question was perfectly fair, and it was only what I had been obsessing about myself. 'He could have been on his way to offer it to somebody else. One of the big dealers. Except that in that case why didn't he go to them before he came here? It was obviously more important than any of the books he asked me to look at.'

My father settled in the other chair and said, 'I want you to think hard about this – as I have been doing for most of the night, as a matter of fact.'

'Barnabas, what's the point? I don't *know* what was going on!'

'But you said that somebody phoned him and he changed his plans abruptly.'

'It could have been anything. The customer changed his mind . . .' As soon as the words were out, I knew they were wrong. If I believe I am going to sell an expensive book to a major customer, and he turns it down at the last minute, I might kick a table leg, but I don't get all sulky and offer it on the internet for five pounds, not unless I'm absolutely desperate for the five pounds.

So Gabriel had been desperate for two thousand pounds.

It would be interesting to know for certain who made the phone call to him. Had it really been somebody saying, 'Ah, Mr Steen, don't bother to keep our appointment because I've changed my mind thank you maybe next time'? I tried to think myself back into that day, when his phone had rung and he had looked at the screen and then rushed out of the shop to speak to the caller. At the time, his behaviour had looked odd, and I'd watched him through the glass of the display window and got the idea that something serious had just happened. He had started to talk about the manuscript as soon as he came back inside. Then he showed it to me, said it was probably valuable. I could almost remember his exact words – he had said, 'Something's come up, I need cash right away.' Offered a deal. And I couldn't turn it down. Maybe I'm a gambler at heart. That had never struck me before.

'Dido?' My father's voice was sharp.

'I'm trying to remember exactly what happened. It's all so confused in my mind. Maybe somebody threatened him. Maybe he needed the cash to pay them off, and when he met them later they wanted more. I wish I'd heard his side of the conversation, but he made sure that I didn't.'

Barnabas made a little sound, a kind of grunt of triumph, and I stared at him hard.

'A threat, then.'

'Maybe. I . . . I guess it could have been.'

'And you have no idea what it was about?'

I was impatient enough to turn on him. 'I keep telling you that!'

'But if it was something about the codex, then was he killing two birds with one stone: getting the cash, getting the thing off his hands?'

'It was an expensive way of doing it!'

'He ended up dead,' Barnabas pointed out. 'If he had thought there was a reasonable chance that it would keep him alive, it wouldn't have seemed too expensive.'

But the police said that Gabriel Steen had been murdered, so if that was his plan, it had failed.

'I'm going to phone Ishmael Peters and tell him to come here. I'll say that the police are asking questions about it. Those Art and Antiquities detectives. I'll say I want to discuss the situation with him.'

Barnabas said, 'I would prefer you to leave detecting to the Essex police force. It is their job.'

I said, 'They seem to be having problems with it at the moment. I suppose they're trying, but I don't get the impression anything's happening. Barnabas, there is one thing I know: I promise you that whoever killed Gabriel Steen, it was *not* Ishmael Peters. Even the police say that, because of his alibi, his being in Amsterdam.'

Barnabas leaned back in his chair and thought about it. 'On the one hand, it could have been a conspiracy in which Peters was involved. On the other hand, there is the fire, suggesting that perhaps Peters was also being threatened.'

'That too,' I agreed. 'But remember, I saw his reaction when I broke the news about Steen's death. He felt guilty – not because of anything he had done but because of something he hadn't done. I'm certain.' And I was. I'd seen the misery in his face, though obviously the police wouldn't look at my instincts as any kind of guidance.

'Then contact him,' Barnabas said abruptly. 'All right: say that you want to talk to him about the codex. But make sure that I'm here when he comes.'

'And Ernie,' I conserted. 'I'll try to get Peters to come here this afternoon. Ernie's due at lunchtime, and I wouldn't bet on Peters in a fight against Ernie. If he comes, I'm going to ask him exactly what happened that day. The problem is, he's a real liar.'

I pulled the beer mat out of the drawer and made the phone call. Ishmael still wasn't answering his mobile, but that didn't surprise me. I left him a message: 'Mr Peters, this is Dido Hoare. Can you come around to the shop this afternoon? I've had some police officers here from Scotland Yard, asking about you and . . . things. I need to talk to you about it. And I'd like your advice about the manuscript. Any time between two and four o'clock is fine with me. I'll be waiting for you.'

119

# Ring-Ring

It was close on three o'clock when the phone rang. I jumped and dropped a book. Acting on instructions, Ernie ignored the call. I could hear Barnabas's footsteps hurrying toward the office door. I grabbed the fallen book off the floor with my right hand, picked up the receiver with my left, and spoke my name.

'Miss Hoare?' a voice asked – a voice with a touch of a Scots accent, not Ishmael Peters. 'This is Harry Mackintosh, Sandbach Books.'

I knew the firm by name, if not the voice, and made polite noises to cover my disappointment.

The voice ploughed on. 'I've had an enquiry from an American collector. Not anybody who's bought from you before, I guess. They've heard that you have a mediaeval codex, and they've asked me to take a look at it and let them know all the details. I was wondering if I could come around this afternoon and look at it?'

I thought very fast and invented a regretful, 'Oh – sorry, it's out on offer.'

Mr Mackintosh was clearly disappointed. 'Oh, well. On offer? You mean . . .'

'I haven't had their decision yet, but these people do have first refusal. I can let you know if they decide not to take it. Uh . . . just in case, would you like to tell me where I can reach you?'

I wrote down the details; we exchanged polite regrets and hung up. Then I took a deep breath and told Barnabas about it.

He stared at me. 'How did Sandbach hear about that thing?'

I was busy checking the details that the caller had given

me with the ABA membership list. Both the address and the telephone number seemed to be correct.

'From their principal?' I suggested. 'Maybe it was advertised by Gabriel at some time? The real question is how they know that we have it now, and the answer to that is—'

'Peters!' Barnabas exploded.

I wasn't sure. 'Or a leak from the police?' I suggested. 'SO1?'

'Very improbable!' Barnabas snorted. 'Not impossible, I grant you, but unlikely.'

There was one way to find out. I dug out my note of the names that the two men had given me, phoned Scotland Yard, and was put through to Sergeant Garner. I simply asked him whether they were in touch with one Harry Mackintosh, or had given my name to any American collector of manuscripts. What I got from him sounded like bewilderment. And then the question whether I had any further information about Ishmael Peters, whom they remained anxious to contact.

'So am I,' I told him shortly. This was getting silly. So it was probably Ishmael who was talking about me to his friends and acquaintances. Why was I surprised? Mr Ishmael Peters wanted money, as much and as soon as possible. It would be a miracle if he weren't marching up and down Piccadilly right now, dressed in a big sandwich board that read, 'For all your mediaeval manuscript needs, contact Miss Dido Hoare at One George Street, Islington.'

But even if he were really walking around with a sign that pointed to me, it gradually became clear that he was not picking up his messages, because four o'clock came and went without a whisper from him.

# End of Day

It couldn't be the hard work in the shop, so it had to be stress. Limp and dizzy, I slumped in the armchair by the fireplace with my eyes shut. The bell in St Mary's tower had just chimed nine o'clock, and I wasn't sure how much longer I could stay awake.

We had stopped waiting for Peters to phone and shut up the shop just after six. I'd fended off Ernie's offer to spend the night on my settee, accepted Barnabas's counter offer to spend some time with Ben, and left the two of them reading in the sitting room while I went unenthusiastically into the kitchen to heat up a tin of vegetable soup and some emergency frozen lasagne. Standing at the door of the kitchen, waiting for the microwave to ping, I listened to the voices from down the hall. They were reading *The Gruffalo* again. Either Ben knew the book by heart now, or Barnabas's reading lessons had been really effective. Either way I wanted to be sitting in there with them. I leaned against the door post, closed my eyes, and tried to feel hungry, without much success. Maybe I was coming down with something.

In the end, I'd managed a small bowl of the soup, picked at some lasagne, and felt well enough for long enough to supervise Ben's bath. The food had helped a little after all, and I'd got Ben into bed at the usual time. Then slumped.

I could hear Barnabas out in the kitchen, rattling the plates and rinsing them under the tap. There was something in the noises he was making which suggested impatience. Apparently if you were in the kitchen they were loud enough to drown out the sound of the doorbell. I pulled myself upright when I heard the buzz, wavered slowly down the stairs, and opened the door.

122

In the darkness of the little sheltered entrance outside, Ishmael Peters was hovering.

'Sorry I'm so late,' he mumbled. 'I got your message. I hope you don't mind me coming now. Couldn't make it any earlier.' He waited, shifting from one foot to the other, and I could smell beer on his breath. Just for the moment I was too exhausted to remember why I'd wanted to see him, but I waved him inside and sent him ahead of me up the stairs. I was awake enough to notice that he seemed to be wobbling almost as much as I was. In the sitting room, he slumped awkwardly on to the settee. I sat stiffly in the chair between him and the door of the room. On guard. What I needed was . . .

'My father was going to make some coffee,' I said. 'It should be ready in a few minutes.'

He was watching me, so I stared back at him in return. I almost asked him what he wanted before I remembered that I was the one who wanted. Wanted him out of my life.

'I saw your lights on up here,' he was saying. 'I'm sorry, you look wiped out, like the English say.'

Do they? I couldn't seem to remember. I sat up straighter and growled, 'Now that you're here I have a couple of questions I want to ask. You've told somebody that I have the manuscript. Who have you told about that, and why?'

I could almost believe that the surprise and alarm were genuine.

'Told? I haven't told anybody.'

I looked at him. He spread his knees, clasped his hands together, and looked up earnestly at Mr Spock who, as I noticed now, was in his favourite spot on the mantelpiece, menacing the visitor with slitted eyes.

I sighed loudly. 'Why should I believe you? I've had a phone call about it. We'll come back to that in a minute. Right now you'd better tell me everything you know about the manuscript. When did you get it? Where? And then everything that you know about what it is.'

'Me? It was Gabe who found—'

'Shut up,' I said. 'I don't believe you.'

'It's true!' he protested. 'It was Gabe who found it at a

123

street stall. When we were in Italy. But Gabe and I were partners. We owned it jointly. We shared everything. But he was the expert. It came from Italy.'

'While Mr Steen was here at the shop that day, you called him on his mobile. What did you say to him, exactly?'

It was a guess, a pure gamble, but it must have been hovering on the edges of my thinking for long enough that it came out in a convincing kind of way. So when I saw him hesitate for a microsecond too long before he started to protest, to deny, I interrupted. 'I was there. I heard the beginning of the call. And Gabriel said something to me about it, you know, something very interesting.'

He looked down at his hands. 'I called to tell him that a guy had been asking questions about it, saying it wasn't really ours. Threatening. I just told Gabe that we needed to get rid of it, get hold of some cash fast.'

I let him see me considering his answer. Nodding reluctantly. 'All right. I suppose that almost makes sense. Now, I'll go back to my last question. Who have you been talking to? Somebody knows that Gabriel gave the thing to me to sell. I've had enquiries.' I could have sworn that an expression of utter panic flashed across his face. I had him cornered. I sat back in my chair and gave him a moment to think it over and realize that fact. Then I said again emphatically, 'Who did you tell?'

'Don't you be a silly girl,' he said unexpectedly. 'Why would I tell anybody? I want *you* to keep it and sell it for every pound or dollar or yen or euro you can get. I need the money. I've lost everything. My life has just been destroyed. I'll have to start again somewhere, and I need cash to do that. We're on the same side, you and me. Why are you—?'

From behind my back, Barnabas's voice interrupted him. 'Who killed Gabriel Steen, then? Was it you? If it wasn't, you certainly know who did it.' My father is twenty years older than Ishmael Peters and has a heart problem which seems to be more or less under control; he is a few inches taller but also a few pounds lighter. I looked at him nervously. And realized that Peters wouldn't stand a chance against my father in this mood.

He slammed the door hard enough to rattle the window panes and stalked across the room towards Peters, who was sitting open-mouthed. 'Tell me,' he commanded. 'Now!'

Peters struggled to rise. By the time he was on his feet, his first panic had subsided.

'I don't know who,' he said. 'I *can't* tell you anything.'

Suddenly he dodged around Barnabas, fumbled at the door knob, and was out of the room. He pulled the door of the flat open, then rattled down the stairs and out. In his hurry, he hadn't stopped to shut that door, either.

'I'll get that,' Barnabas said. 'For a moment I thought . . . Never mind. Are you ready for your coffee? One small cup. Then I'm going too. Bed for you.'

I wasn't sure about the coffee, but perhaps it could keep me awake long enough for the five-minute post-mortem with Barnabas that I badly needed. But I admit that I was asleep on my feet, and that's my only excuse for not knowing, not asking, the right question. I *was* sure that Ishmael Peters knew who had killed his friend, his partner, whatever the two of them had been; although the knowledge didn't seem to be doing him any good.

# The Book Business

As Barnabas says, when business is slow you just have to try a little harder.

We were all in the shop: my father and me, Ben, Ernie, even a customer or two who had included bookshops in their Saturday morning shopping trek. Ben was temporary, having a lunchtime engagement with a friend from his nursery school. I'd drive him down to the Smiths' place in Finsbury in a little while. In the meantime Barnabas was somehow keeping him occupied and also dealing with customers. Ernie and I were putting in some time on the new catalogue. We had worked out a routine over the past couple of years. Ernie was presenting me with short print-outs from our website listings; I was checking the items to make sure they were still available and that the descriptions didn't need amendment. When necessary, Ernie was amending. Amendments usually had to do with prices. Occasionally I looked something up in an auction catalogue and added a few pounds to the previous listed price; or subtracted a few. I was also deleting items, if something had already been sold, and checking the condition of the more valuable things that were out on the shelves.

Just at the moment I was in the process of discovering that one book was mysteriously missing, apparently stolen. Considering that I had it priced at four pounds, I was prepared to console myself for its loss, though not until I had made sure that it wasn't mis-shelved. I searched without much hope, though, because I thought I knew who had stolen the thing on account of the fact that, according to the website entry, it was a 'British Library paperback, excellent condition, undated,' entitled *Magic in Medieval Manuscripts*. I had a kind of resigned feeling that Ishmael Peters had outwitted me some time recently when my back was turned. I told Ernie to delete it from the catalogue listing but not the site. I might get it back. Or I might just keep it listed as a permanent reminder not to trust some people.

'What's wrong?' Barnabas demanded, appearing in the doorway with a book in one hand and a credit card in the other.

'Can't find a book,' I grunted, and wrapped the volume for him while he was dealing with the credit card payment.

He changed the subject. 'Maybe you should only open at the weekends?'

'Maybe it will get better. The American dealers will start coming back in another couple of months.'

Ernie said, 'One of our lecturers says soon everything'll be internet sales.'

Barnabas snorted. He liked to feel the quality with his own fingers. I could understand both attitudes.

Ben said, 'Can we go now?' In the last couple of months his clock-reading had become impeccable. We pulled ourselves together and left.

His luncheon engagement was only a ten-minute drive to the south. When I got back less than half an hour later, my parking space had been taken. I slowed and drove obediently up and down the nearby streets, because on Saturdays the traffic wardens are everywhere, and business wasn't brisk enough to justify paying another parking fine. I was three streets away before I found a space. I hurried back, keeping my eyes peeled for any sight of Ishmael Peters's bulky body. But I was lucky today.

Back in the shop I found Ernie hunched over the computer, and Barnabas staring over his shoulder reading what was on the screen.

'We got two hundred and sixty-one entries,' Ernie announced to me. 'Should be sixty pages, Dido. That enough?'

'It'll do. We can fill up some space with black-and-white illustrations.' Issuing a catalogue, especially a catalogue of illustrated books, you can include as many pictures of the choicest pieces as you want or can afford to, because after all that's the point of it all, and the strategy pays off.

Barnabas said, 'Lunchtime. Ernie . . . ?'

Ernie agreed that he wouldn't mind a kebab, and would be back in twenty minutes.

After the door had closed behind him, leaving Barnabas and me and two female customers alone in the shop, Barnabas muttered, 'Is all well?'

'We got there safely. She'll phone when it's time for me to go and get him.'

My father threw an ironic glance in my direction. 'I assumed as much. What I intended, however, was to ask whether you have recovered from last night?'

I hadn't really stopped to think about last night, but now that he mentioned it . . . 'I asked Peters the wrong question.'

Barnabas looked at me sharply: explanation required.

'Barnabas, he didn't kill Steen, they know that. You asked him whether he knew who did . . .'

'And he lied. He does know. Knows something, certainly. It was as plain as the nose on your face.'

I struggled to explain. 'What I thought he does know is something else about the manuscript. He keeps saying that Gabriel found it, Gabriel owned it, it was Gabriel who knew all about it. But even if that were true, Gabriel must have told him everything he knew about it. Barnabas, think about this! Something as old and wonderful and valuable as that? They would have sat there in Gabriel's flat looking at it and talking about it and getting all excited. So why does he think he can't tell me what he knows?'

'Perhaps he doesn't like women. Pushy women.' I imitated Barnabas's personal look of wise cynicism, the one which he must have practised on generations of students over the decades. 'No? Very well, then what?' Barnabas asked.

'This morning, I realized that I never asked him the right question. I asked him who he'd told about my having the manuscript, and I know that he was lying about that. Then I asked him what *he* knew about it, about what it is. I did ask him why he phoned Gabriel Steen that day and what he said to him, but I made a mistake. I didn't insist enough, so

128

he never told me the truth. Whatever it was, it sent Steen running. And Peters is the only person alive who knows the truth.'

Barnabas looked bewildered. 'He was the one who phoned?'

'I think so. I'm almost sure.' Peters wasn't very good at hiding the truth. It did seem fairly likely that I'd get another chance to ask, though I couldn't be sure because Peters's behaviour was so erratic. He could vanish in a flash if he decided that he was in as much danger as Gabriel had been, and obviously this was a complication.

'Go upstairs,' Barnabas said abruptly. 'Ernie will be back in a minute. Make a pot of tea and get yourself some food. I'll join you shortly. Is there anything in particular that you must do here this afternoon?'

'I'll take some photos,' I said. 'For the catalogue.'

'And I will deal with customers and make a few suggestions about things that Ernie might look up via the internet. In between holding up books to the camera, of course.'

At that point the two women wandered towards the office to pay for a copy of one of Cecil Aldin's sentimental dog books, cheap because of a torn illustration. I'd better try to remember to check whether this one had been included in the catalogue, though some of us think that having a few items already sold before a catalogue is actually issued just makes purchasers eager to act more promptly next time. It's psychology.

# New Best Friend

M aybe he had been in the shop the day before while I was out, because I didn't know the man when he came in during our short opening hours on Sunday, but Ernie recognized him.

He looked around casually, as though familiar with the place, and then started taking books off the shelves at the front of the shop, looking at the titles and one or two of the other pages, and then putting them back and sliding to his left. What made me watch him was the fact that his actions were repetitive. He was moving at an even pace from one book to the next, all of them shelved at eye level but not all the same kind of book. He left the strong impression of not really seeing any of them. Neither book collectors nor present-seekers nor readers behave like that.

I moved into a spot from which I could watch him in the security mirror. I was waiting to see something vanishing into a pocket, or the zipped front of his navy blue rain jacket, at which moment Ernie and I would go out and surround him and kindly give him the opportunity to change his mind. But he wasn't interested in books, not even free books.

At some point I became aware of the fact that Ernie in turn was watching me. I held up a finger, pointed, and whispered, 'I'll just go and ask that man whether I can help him. Shh!'

Ernie nodded, but he followed me out of the office and drifted towards the door to the street. Good idea. I went the other way, wandered around the end of the rear bookcase, and smiled sweetly.

'Hello. Can I show you anything?'

'Just looking,' he said calmly and finally. He went on

pulling another volume off the shelf in front of him and again scanned the title page.

I took the opportunity to look more closely at him. I was thinking that some time I might be asked to describe him: about forty-five or fifty, mid-brown hair cut short, weather-beaten face, clean-shaven, blue eyes, blue jeans, black trainers. Very ordinary.

He glanced at me. 'You the owner?'

I nodded.

'Very nice book shop.' He had some kind of northern accent, probably Geordie, but not very strong. There was something about him, about his manner and his confidence, that seemed familiar, and yet I couldn't identify it at first. Then he replaced the last volume, nodded at me again, turned, and marched past Ernie and out of the shop.

'Copper,' Ernie said as soon as the door had shut behind him.

'Do you think so?' I said, but I didn't disagree. Maybe that was what I'd seen in his actions too: confidence, not caring what anybody thought.

Ernie was scowling. 'Dido, I think he was here yesterday, but he was sitting outside in a car when I saw him. I thought he was waiting for somebody. He didn't come in.'

'Maybe they sent him to watch for Mr Peters after all,' I suggested. 'Never mind, he's gone now.' Or he had just given that impression. 'Ernie? If you do see him here again, remember to tell me.'

We closed at four o'clock on the dot. I paid Ernie, and we went out together and parted at the corner. I had a small bundle of cash and cheques to deposit in the night safe at my bank, and I was just turning into Upper Street when my mobile phone rang. I took refuge from the wind against a shop window to asnwer it.

It was Ernie's voice: 'Dido? He's still here.'

'Who's where?' I demanded anxiously.

'The copper. I just saw him sitting in a car just up the street from th' shop. Wait – he's turning the engine on. Lights. He's going now.'

I said quickly, 'Ernie, can you get the car's registration?'

'Yeah.' I listened to a moment's silence, and then his voice came again: 'Got it. He's making a left, Essex Road direction.'

I was scrabbling in my pocket and failed to find a pen or for that matter anything to write on, barring the envelope I was about to post in the night safe. 'Text it to me now!' I hissed. 'Ernie, thank you.'

I switched off and completed my errand at a jog, not just because I was in a hurry to join Ben and Barnabas, who would soon get back from visiting the pet monkey belonging to my father's upstairs neighbour, but because I wanted to pick up the policeman's registration number – if he was a policeman. I wouldn't be able to do anything about that until tomorrow morning, when Laura Smiley would probably be on duty. I was pretty sure she'd be willing to tell me what was going on. After all, she was the one who had begged me to contact her if anything happened. In the meantime I felt like shutting myself into the flat to do harmless and boring things like wiping down the counter tops in the kitchen or slumping in front of the TV.

# PI

When I came back from the nursery walk, I went upstairs into the flat. And as I had been anticipating, the phone rang promptly at nine thirty.

'Hello, Ms Hoare. Laura Smiley here.'

I had managed to catch her earlier, just as she came on duty, to tell her about the mysterious watcher. She had promised to run his registration number and report back.

'I think you can stop worrying. It's not us, though you were right that the man is . . . actually, *was* . . . a policeman; he's retired now. He's working for a firm in Enfield called David Martin Investigations.'

'A . . . a private eye?'

I heard her laugh. 'Yes, all right. The firm is genuine, by the way. I phoned them and talked to Mr Martin himself. I told them that a lady in Islington had made a complaint about somebody stalking her – I hope you don't mind.'

*Mind being called a lady?* 'What did he say?'

'That they've been hired to trace a person who owes their client some money. He told them that this person might have a connection with your shop. Mr Nicholl was assigned to the job, and he has apparently been hanging around off and on for the past three days.'

Considering the number of shoppers and commuters in the area, it looked as though we'd noticed him pretty promptly. As for the rest of the story . . . 'Did they tell you who they're after?'

'You might not be surprised to hear that they're looking for a Mr Ishmael Peters?'

No, I wasn't very surprised. I could easily imagine Peters skipping out on a debt.

'Who hired them?' I demanded eagerly. It didn't work.

'I didn't even ask, because I was sure he would prefer not to tell me. That kind of thing is regarded as confidential in any decent agency, unless it's an official police request of course. So I just informed him that the Serious Crimes Unit are also interested in that person's whereabouts, and that if they locate him he should give us the full details immediately. I've already warned SO1 about what's been happening over there, so I think they'll reinforce my message.'

I wondered aloud what *was* going on.

She laughed. 'If you don't know, I don't suppose anybody else does.'

At that point I remembered to thank her sincerely for her help. I couldn't think of anything else to say, but now she was the one who was hesitating.

'Ms Hoare, I'm sure it's nothing to worry about – really.'

I returned her hesitation. 'All right.'

'But if you see him again, and he's worrying you at all, perhaps you'd like to phone me? If I'm not tied up with something else, I'll come straight over there and let him know who I am, and that we are aware. His boss is going to tell him that I got in touch, I'm sure, but I'm happy to let him know we're keeping an eye open.'

Never turn down an offer of backup is my motto. I thanked her even more warmly. We said our goodbyes, and then I wandered into the kitchen to get a coffee, and back to the sitting room to drink it and try to think. The second part of that operation was so fruitless that I was actually relieved when Barnabas interrupted me with his usual morning phone call. I told him that Ben had enjoyed seeing the monkey yesterday, and that I was going to spend the day doing the laundry and keeping out of trouble. He seemed to approve.

# Dealings

An hour later, I was sitting in the little launderette around the corner. My two machine loads were going round and round in a boring way, encouraging idle thought. I'd decided not to worry about Mr Nicholl. If I saw him again I might just ask him a few questions about his work. The funny thing was that his interest and mine were probably more or less the same. After all, we both needed to know where Ishmael Peters was hanging out. My desire was probably less antagonistic than his, though.

The nearest washing machine stopped, waited, and reversed its drum. Maybe I ought to try to find him before the others did? That seemed a dubious notion, but I was beginning to feel oppressed by the importance of my question, the one that I hadn't worked out until it was too late to make him give me the real complete answer instead of a half answer: *What did you say to Gabriel when you spoke to him that day?*

Maybe a better idea would be to tag on to the coat-tails of the professionals. I could phone Alan Quinn. Couldn't I? At least I knew him. I still hadn't worked out why he had seemed less forthcoming the last time we'd spoken. I just wanted him to realize that questioning Ishmael Peters was in fact a part of his own job.

I must have let out a little groan of impatience, because the woman who ran the launderette, and who was wandering towards the door with a packet of cigarettes in her hand, stopped beside me long enough to say, 'It's all right, the machine's just finishing. You can get that first load into the dryer now.'

'Thanks,' I said. But I delayed the transfer for another

minute or two while I tried to get a strong enough signal for my mobile phone. I gave up for a minute or two in order to sling my damp laundry from one machine to another and insert a couple of coins in the slot. Then I joined her outside, moved a little way up the street, and tried Chris Kennedy's mobile. Sometimes I am very jealous of Chris. Because he is a journalist, he can ask things of policemen that I can't. To be more exact, he can get the answers I don't. His phone was on, and he answered at once.

'Dido? Hi. I can't talk for long, I'm just going into an editorial meeting. Are you all right?'

'I'm all right,' I told him a little uncertainly, 'but I need your help. It's complicated, but I need you to bully Alan Quinn for me.'

'You mean you want me to do my "it's-not-me-it's-my-newspaper– sir" act?'

I stopped myself laughing and told him yes.

'Then suppose I come by the shop in about two hours to get your instructions?'

'If I'm not in the shop I'll be either upstairs or out trailing a suspect,' I told him. 'Watch out for me in a trench coat and a trilby hat.'

He said, 'I'll be looking forward to it. If I like the hat, I'll take you out to lunch.'

Chris switched off his phone and said, 'He listened. I'm not sure that it did much good.'

I told him that I'd understood that much.

Chris had come up with his own story: that the more research he did for his piece on Gabriel Steen, the more he kept hearing about Steen's involvement with an American expatriate by the name of Ishmael Peters, and that he had heard the police were asking questions about this man. Who was Peters, then? Did they know how to get in touch with him?

It had sounded from the side of the conversation I'd heard that he was being given the same old story I'd already had: SO1 were pursuing that lead, while in Essex they were confining their investigations to Steen's London visit and its culmination in his death.

'SO1?' he'd asked. 'Serious crime? What, we've got some international gangsters on bicycles? . . . Oh, I see. Art theft.' He had held up a finger at me. 'This Peters – I know he's a painter, I got a look at his website a couple of days ago, and . . . Yes, of course. Any idea whether he's still in London?' There had been a long silence at that point while he'd listened without speaking, then he had said, 'As a matter of fact, Dido Hoare says that he's been around to her shop a couple of times – she's not sure why – and he wouldn't give her any information except that he was going to stay in London for the time being. She thinks he knows more about Steen's death than he's saying. She's decided that he must be the one who phoned Steen while he was with her, the day he died . . . No, I don't know. Just an impression she got from something he said, I think. Yes, you're right, they might know more about him . . . SO1? . . . Right, I've got those names. I'll give one of them a ring. Thanks, Alan, and good luck with this whole business.'

He switched off and we looked at each other.

'Did you get that?'

I thought I probably had. 'It didn't do much good, did it?'

'They've been warned,' he said thoughtfully. 'If something happens that reminds them of that, they'll act on what they've heard. They are professionals.'

'*And* they don't forget it,' I said sourly.

'I don't see the hat,' he said slowly, 'but I'll take you out to lunch anyway if you like. Only I have to be back at the paper by three thirty.'

The alternative was for me to go downstairs and work on the catalogue. No contest.

# Message

When I got back at three thirty, I knew that I was feeling interested enough at last to go into the shop for an hour and do a little work. The morning's post was still lying in a small heap under the letter slot, but aside from that everything seemed to be under control. I turned off the security system, swept into the office and switched on the desk light. The answering machine was blinking. I grabbed a pen and a notepad and prepared to deal with it.

First message: the voice was unfamiliar at first, but it identified the speaker as Terence Fletcher. He had rung at nine o'clock and was anxious for me to ring him back. Barnabas was the second: 'Dido? . . . You must be upstairs.' Also the third: 'Your phone seems to be engaged.' The fourth was Dr Fletcher again: 'I may have some news for you.' To my amazement, the next was a request to buy a book, and when I checked I found the volume there on the shelf. I returned to the office with it, placed it prominently on the packing table with a note of the purchaser, and continued. The final call was from Dr Fletcher again, a longer message this time. When I had listened through to the end, I replayed it and paid closer attention.

'Miss Hoare, I'm sorry you aren't back. I've been searching the internet and making a few phone calls, and I think I've found something. I'm leaving work now. Since you aren't in today, I wonder whether you could phone me first thing in the morning?'

I tried to read the things that he wasn't actually saying, but I couldn't be sure whether it was excitement or something more like disappointment that I was hearing in his voice. Because of it, I phoned the British Library anyway and was told that Dr Fletcher had already left and couldn't be reached.

He had probably spoken to Barnabas. But when I tried my father's number, I got no response. Maybe the news I wasn't going to like had required him to go out and do something about it. However, since he absolutely refused ever to keep the mobile phone that I'd given him switched on, there was nothing I could do to find out.

I wrote out an invoice, put that and the book into a padded envelope, printed out an address label and attached it very neatly, and then slid it into my shoulder bag. If I walked it over to the post office and sent it off before I went on to the nursery, I could even claim that my day hadn't been entirely without profit.

It was after four thirty by the time I was ready to leave. I locked up, threw an automatic glance overhead at the security lights which were flashing above the door to show that the system was set, and turned around.

The car was there again on the other side of the road. I could see the number plate, which was still just readable despite the growing darkness.

The sky overhead was black with clouds. It was going to rain again in a little while. I pretended to consult my wristwatch and hesitate. All right. I started to cross the road in a diagonal track that would take me over to the other pavement at a point behind his car, but at the proper moment I swerved suddenly and stopped at the driver's door. I was right: somebody was sitting inside. I leaned my left hand on the roof of the car and twirled my right hand in the universal sign: Roll your window down.

It rolled.

I leaned over a little, staring him in the eye, and said, 'Good evening, Mr Nicholl. I take it that you haven't spoken to Mr Martin recently?'

He froze for a minute, then opened his door slowly and got out. 'Miss Hoare? I'm sorry, I didn't hear what you said.'

I shook my head at him in disgust. 'Really? What I said was, "Hello, Mr Nicholl, I take it you haven't spoken to your employer recently?"'

He stared.

I said, 'You're in a residents' parking bay, you know. Us residents find that very annoying. Anyway, you'd better phone in.'

'You have a message for me?'

'Not exactly,' I told him comfortably, still looking him in the eye. 'You'll find a public phone in Upper Street. Turn right, and it's just up on the right.'

I gave him a curt nod, turned around, and headed toward the cross street just to make it clear that I had taken the trouble to make a little detour in order to deliver a message that he would be needing, and obviously I knew all about him. He wouldn't have told me anything, even if I'd asked.

By the time that Ben and I got home, the car was gone.

# Conspiracy

The phone in the office was ringing as I got back next morning to open up. I rushed inside and broke into the answering machine's outgoing message just as it was winding up.

'Hell-lo, Dido?' It was Ernie. 'Lecturers' strike today. I just remembered. It's all day, so do you want me to come in?'

'Are you sure you shouldn't be studying or something?' I asked him suspiciously.

'I c'd do a bit of work on your computer, if you don't mind. I've got a project designing a font texturizer, but I've got my files backed up on my flash drive, so I c'd do that and work on the catalogue the rest of the time?'

I avoided asking him what language he was speaking because, considering the number of pieces of unfinished business left over from yesterday, I thought that having some backup might be wise, even if it was busy texturizing. I agreed with haste.

While I was at the phone, I decided to deal with yesterday's callers, starting with Barnabas.

He answered promptly. 'Dido – good! You got my message?'

'I tried to ring you back yesterday, but—'

'No, no, a little while ago. Upstairs. Are you in the shop, then?'

I explained that I was, and that Ernie and I would be here together for most of the day if he wanted to go and do something else again.

'Have you heard from Dr Fletcher?' I added. 'He left a couple of messages on my answering machine yesterday, but

141

he'd left work by the time I was able to pick them up. I was going to phone him next.'

'Ah. Yes. In fact, he spoke to me yesterday afternoon because he hadn't heard from you. He wants you to go in and get the codex, this afternoon at the latest. You'd better make your phone call. Oh – and warn Mr Stockton that you're bringing it back to him.'

I hadn't expected this. It took me a moment to pull myself together and ask, 'Why?'

'It appears that . . . no, I'd better let him explain in person. In fact, I think I'll catch the bus down there in a few minutes and go with you. Wait for me.'

The next task was to contact Fletcher himself and try to find out what was going on.

He stammered, 'I-I've stumbled across something I – well, I wasn't expecting. I need to show you. I spoke to Professor Hoare yesterday, but I need to show you for yourself.'

He sounded so peculiar that I wanted to scream at him for a proper explanation. But I got hold of myself and left it, just told him that I would be turning up as soon as I could get away. Then I spent some time checking catalogue items and confirming prices while I waited for everyone to get there.

Ernie was first. By the time I had finished showing him which material I had proof-read and which I hadn't, Barnabas was at the door. I went to meet him. Before I locked up again, I stepped outside for a casual look up and down the street. The detective's car didn't seem to be there. Perhaps all that business was actually finished. Or he might have changed cars. The street was rainy and quiet, almost re-assuringly normal, and I even started to wonder whether I'd been imagining things.

'Do you know what it is that Dr Fletcher found?' I asked Barnabas as we made our way back into the office.

'He told me he may have located a manuscript which is closer to Gabriel Steen's codex than anything else we have seen. It's in the United States. Dr Fletcher says there has been much discussion of it on the internet in past years, and he was expecting to have located some pictures of it by this morning. He wants to show them to us as soon as possible.'

That sounded good to me, and I wasn't sure why I was getting signals that both Barnabas and Dr Fletcher were deeply uneasy about something. Presumably our conference would make all that clear. While I remembered, I phoned Leonard Stockton's office and left a message with his secretary that we would be arriving later today with a valuable object for safe-keeping. Then I opened the final two envelopes, dropped their contents on to the packing table, and phoned for a taxi.

Fletcher met us at the reception desk with a strained smile on his face.

Barnabas noticed it too and reacted by becoming reassuring and fatherly. He got in first: 'Dr Fletcher, I hope you're well?'

'Thank you, yes. Will you come upstairs?'

Without waiting for a response, he turned on his heel and strode towards the staircase. My father and I exchanged glances. It had been more like a command than an invitation. Barnabas ostentatiously offered me his arm. I ostentatiously took it, and we followed our guide at a pace which was businesslike, but required him to slow down if he didn't want to lose us in his dust.

'He seems edgy,' Barnabas muttered unnecessarily. 'Something's happened here.'

'He'd better not have lost it,' I muttered back.

Barnabas sighed. 'Just don't . . .' But by that time our guide had let us catch him up, and he had to stop what he was saying.

Fletcher slammed his office door behind us. 'Sit down, sit down, I have something to show you.'

'The test results?'

'Oh . . . sorry, not yet. They promised something by next week. But this arrived yesterday afternoon. Wait, I'll turn it around so we can all look at it.'

'It' was his computer screen. We sat on a cramped row of chairs along the front of his desk; he leant forward and clicked his mouse, and the screen came to life revealing a sombre grey background on which a number of icons were showing. Another click, and the e-mail came to life. He fiddled with the mouse, located the one that he wanted, opened the file, and found an attachment to the message. At that point, he hesitated.

'I've been discussing your problem with a friend at the Beinecke Library in New Haven,' he said abruptly. 'I sent him a few of your digital pictures last Friday and asked him whether they looked at all familiar to him, and he found . . . I'll show you what he found.'

The attachment opened out into an image of a yellowish document. The centre of the picture was surrounded by narrow white margins. At first I thought I was looking at something which was displayed on a piece of white paper, but then I saw that it was just a reproduction of an illustration in an ordinary modern book, with some of the margins showing. More important than what it was, was what the image showed. A drawing of a number of plump naked women sitting in a large octagonal bathtub filled the top two thirds of the page, while the bottom third contained four or five lines of the familiar brown-ink script with the exaggerated right-hand loops. Barnabas and I both leaned forward.

I whispered, 'Can you read it?'

Barnabas said loudly, 'Of course not. No more than you can.' He reared back and looked at Fletcher. 'What is this?'

Instead of answering him, Fletcher clicked back up to the beginning of the file. Images flew past so quickly that it I couldn't focus on anything specific, just saw that they contained more of the familiar kind of pictures. Then the title page appeared: we were looking at book called *The Telschi Conspiracy* by Alan Jenkins and Ethel Glass.

'Do you have a copy of this book in the collection here?' Barnabas asked.

'No, it was published in New York in 1962, and it doesn't seem to have been on sale in this country. The New York Public Library had a copy at one time, but the records say that the item was deleted from the catalogue in 1990.'

'Who owns this copy?' I asked hopefully.

'The Library of Congress.'

'More to the point,' Barnabas said impatiently, 'where is the original of this manuscript?'

Fletcher shrugged. 'A collection in Texas, I think.'

'Which? Where?'

Fletcher shook his head, frowning. 'I'm not sure. But some of the references mention that the Telschi manuscript is in private hands now, that's the point. The photographic reproductions, insofar as they exist, were made public before the manuscript was sold to the present owner. Nobody seems to have published any new information for some time, and it doesn't seem very easy to get permission to visit the collection.'

'Why does this book talk about a "conspiracy"?' I wondered aloud.

They both looked at me. Fletcher shook his head.

'Well. Thank you for your help,' Barnabas said suddenly. 'You have spent a good deal of time on this, and I really am most grateful. Perhaps we should get back to the shop now, if you could let us have our codex?'

I was expecting to be escorted down to the safe room again, but today was different. Dr Fletcher nodded almost eagerly, and pulled out the little book from a locked drawer in one of his filing cabinets, along with the big envelope which contained our digital photos of its folios. He looked happy to be getting rid of the whole business, and I noticed that he was being much less careful than last time about how he handled the volume. I took the little manuscript from him, placed it in the envelope for protection, and slid it inside my shoulder bag and out of sight. Then I saw that Barnabas was sitting unmoving in his chair, staring at the computer screen. That gave me an idea.

'Could you please let me have a copy of that e-mail?'

Fletcher said, 'Please, of course, you just forward the whole thing to your own e-mail address. Go ahead.'

I sat down a little awkwardly at his desk and did as he had suggested. As soon as I stood up again and moved away, he sprang to erase the whole file without even stopping to sit down. Then he smiled like somebody who had just been cured of a migraine headache. It was all over the top, but I couldn't think how to persuade him to tell us what was wrong.

Nor could Barnabas, because he got quietly to his feet and thanked Fletcher again, and then Fletcher showed us out. We had barely taken a step down the corridor before we heard the lock on his door snap.

Barnabas put a strong hand on my arm and urged me back towards the staircase without speaking.

I said, 'What?'

'He thinks our manuscript is a forgery, that's what it is: a copy of this Telschi thing, presumably. He wasn't sure whether we already knew that. Let's just go and find a taxi, for goodness sake, and get back to the shop. There are usually some cabs at the rank around the corner. Lord help us!'

We followed that plan. Later, when we got out of the taxi by the shop, I left Barnabas to pay while I scanned the parked cars and went over to unlock the door, where I discovered that there were no lights on inside. As far as anybody could actually see in the darkness, there was no Ernie. I told myself that he might have gone out to get himself some lunch, although, even after our detour to leave the manuscript in safe hands, it was still not quite noon. And how did he plan to get back in until we turned up? I wondered uneasily whether something had happened at the nursery.

146

# Following Ishmael

'I'm going to phone and make sure that Ben's all right,' I said to Barnabas, who had been either sitting at the computer ever since our return, or pacing up and down one of the aisles in the front in silent thought. Fletcher's e-mail had arrived and my father had spent twenty minutes examining the file, shot by shot.

Luckily for everybody's temper, the telephone rang at that very moment and when I snatched up the receiver I could hear Ernie's voice. My heart was pounding in my ears. I got hold of myself.

'Ernie,' I said, 'what happened?'

'My battery's going flat.' It was barely audible. 'Look, that old American? He came and rang the bell just after you left. I di'n't budge and he went away again, but I know you want to pin him down, so I grabbed my jacket and came out after him.' His voice crackled and seemed to fade for a moment, and the next word that I heard clearly was, 'Wembley.'

'You're in Wembley?' I said frantically. '*He's* in Wembley? Where?'

There was another second or two of the fading voice, but I caught the words 'Elsley Road, number twenty, just . . . tube station . . .' There was one last moment of power in which I heard, 'Outa money.'

Was he saying that he was penniless and marooned in Wembley?

I shrieked, 'I'm coming! Stay there!' just before I lost the connection altogether.

My father had heard the shrieking and came to stand in the office doorway. I caught my breath and said, 'Ernie. He

147

saw Ishmael Peters outside and decided to follow him. He managed to give me an address in Wembley just before his battery went flat. I think he said that he doesn't have any money on him. Barnabas, I'll have to drive over and pick him up. Please could you stay here by the phone in case he finds a payphone or something and rings again? If he does, tell him I'm on my way to Elsley Road. I'll leave my mobile on in case you need to get a message to me, and I'll phone you as soon as I find out what's going on.'

'You might,' he said drily as I was pushing past him, 'ring me anyway in, say, half an hour? Whether you've located Ernie or not? Just to let me know that you haven't crashed the purple monster and are therefore still conscious?'

I waved to him and rushed out towards the 'purple monster' – my big MPV. I've had it for several years, and it's a perfectly sensible multi-purpose vehicle for a bookseller to run; but for some reason my father is always sarcastic about the colour. From Islington to Wembley takes a mere half hour in the middle of a Tuesday. The rain fell faster and harder as the minutes passed, and before long I was throwing up sheets of water whenever I bumped into a pothole or crashed through the overflow from a blocked drain. I pulled off the North Circular at the Harrow Road, stopped to look at the street atlas in the glove compartment, and eventually located Elsley Road, zigzagged up to it, and rolled gently past the face of number twenty. The house was one of a row of old brick three-storey semi-detached houses. I passed it without slowing and pulled up outside number forty-six, which seemed far enough away for me not to be visible. I left the engine and the wipers on, wondering what to do.

Then there was movement in my rear-view mirror, and Ernie came scrambling into the passenger seat with water running off his nose and leather jacket, saying, 'He's still there. It's been raining so hard, you wouldn't want go out.'

I wondered aloud what we ought to do. Then I realized that I could put off making any decisions for the time being, because the big blue umbrella which I keep behind my seat would provide me with cover of more than one kind.

'Wait here,' I said.

'I better come with you.'

I searched for inspiration and explained, 'I think this is the proper technique when you're shadowing somebody: you change places with your partner often enough that they won't notice what's going on.' I didn't want Peters to become aware of us until I'd made up my mind what to do about him. I got out, put up the umbrella, held it down low over my head and walked back.

It was scarcely worth taking care. The house, as I passed it, looked neglected and crumbling. The hard rain was overflowing the gutters – there was a kind of waterfall over the front entrance where a downfall pipe had been blocked. I might have been worried that the house was empty except that I could just detect some dim lights glowing behind two of the windows. As I walked past the front steps I tilted the umbrella far enough to be able to see that there was a panel of eight or ten doorbells beside the chipped black door. I could also see that none of them had name cards beside them. If you were visiting somebody in this place, you would have to know which tiny flatlet was your destination.

Somehow it seemed a bad idea to walk up the path and ring all the bells in turn in the hope that the residents would come and attend an identity parade. Besides, it was the sort of place where half of them wouldn't work. The bells, that is. Well, possibly the residents too.

The curtains in the ground floor bay were drawn together tight, but light leaked out around the top edges. A torn scrap of fabric dangled from the corner of one dirty curtain, and they looked as though they had all been scavenged from somebody's recycling bin. Just in case Peters happened to be inside looking out at the rain, I walked well past without pausing, crossed the road, and stood under the partial shelter of a tree to think things over. This would be the right place. It was just the sort of house where someone like Ishmael Peters, or an impoverished student or an out-of-work sales assistant on benefit, would take refuge. It didn't look like the kind of place where the landlord would ask for references: a couple of weeks' rent in advance would probably be enough to get you in.

149

The only problem was how I could make sure of it without warning him.

I splashed back to the car, collapsed the umbrella and threw it into the rear footwell to drain, then dived quickly into the front seat.

'See him?' Ernie asked.

I said no, but I wasn't worried.

Time was passing. I started the car and pulled out, made a U-turn and drove soberly back past number twenty. 'The house looks as though it's divided into cheap studio flats,' I started to explain. I was interrupted by the sound of my ring tone. Barnabas.

'Sorry,' I said before he had a chance to complain. 'I was out of the car for a few minutes, I've only just got back.'

'Well?' Barnabas demanded.

'I'm pretty sure that he's renting a room here. It isn't a hotel or anything like that, so he might be using another name, paying cash, and not planning on staying for very long. Especially if I do the wrong thing and scare him off.'

Barnabas said, 'If Ernie –'

'He's here,' I assured him. 'I've picked him up.'

'Then you can bring him back with you and phone the police from the shop,' Barnabas said sharply. 'I take it you'll be back well before five?'

'Barring accidents,' I said. 'If anything delays us, I'll phone you. Will you be there, or upstairs?'

'Upstairs,' he growled. 'I need a cup of tea. I don't suppose there's any food?'

It didn't take a genius to guess that something was wrong. 'There's probably something in the fridge. I'm going to be turning on to the North Circular in a minute, so I'll switch off now.'

Ernie suggested that he would like to use my car's phone charger. I agreed and turned the wipers on to maximum and the heater to three-quarters. Ernie attached his dead phone to my charger, leaned back, shut his eyes, and started to hum.

We found a half-mile tailback ahead of us as we were approaching the A1 junction and had to slow to an intermittent crawl. It gave me the chance to think. By this time I

150

was regretting not ringing all the doorbells in the house, if necessary, until Ishmael Peters came out. The trouble was that I couldn't quite decide what I was going to say when I did finally face him. I might have only one chance before he slipped away again. 'Ishmael Peters, tell me why you keep hanging around?', 'Ishmael Peters, you are under citizen's arrest on a charge of being a stinking nuisance?', 'Ishmael Peters, what did you say when you phoned Gabriel Steen the day he was killed?'

Well, yes, that last one . . . as though there was any chance that he'd tell me the truth.

Or there was the easy option: the one where I would simply contact New Scotland Yard and give his current address to a grateful team of hard-boiled coppers who were already looking for him. Part of me would just relax if that worked; the other half would feel sorry for him, or something stupid like that. I should probably sleep on the problem.

But I saw quite soon that at this rate of progress I wasn't going to get to the nursery in time to pick Ben up. I postponed the problem by asking Ernie to use my mobile and warn Barnabas that we were still floating towards Hampstead Garden suburb. That done, we had a short and fruitless discussion about what to do. It was getting dark. Assuming that my business was selling books, it had been a spectacularly wasted day. I didn't even bother to ask, just made a quick left turn and delivered Ernie to his mother's house up Hendon way before I looped around and came down from the north against the rush-hour traffic, and got home at about the time that Ben and Barnabas had finished eating and were grumbling to each other about the weather and my absence.

My son threw himself on me with hugs. My father, on the other hand, sat back and glared. Somehow I got the impression that only Ben's presence was preventing a serious scolding and possibly a smack on the hand. As it was, he confined himself to asking whether I thought I was Sherlock Holmes. Or perhaps Inspector Clouseau? I said no, it was simply that Ernie had been being Philip Marlowe, but without Marlowe's financial backing, which puzzled him.

# Clear as a Cloud

The bright spot, next morning, was the weather: the rain had stopped. There had been pictures on the television news last evening of underpasses in west London flooded so deep that double-decker buses were stuck under the bridges, but this morning the clouds were thinner and from time to time the sun tried to break through.

I didn't even bother to go into the shop. Apart from opening the mail, if there was any and if I could make the effort, I couldn't see that it mattered. Oh. Finishing the catalogue, getting it ready for printing? Ernie was due at lunchtime. We'd do it then. I went upstairs, drank the rest of my breakfast pot of coffee, and tried to think things through.

Barnabas has a method for this kind of thing. On the occasions when he faces a complex problem, he writes everything down, shifts the elements around, frowns at them and makes the connections. I found a pad of fuschia-coloured sticky notes, and wrote one or two things on one or two pieces until the first one, the one which said 'Catch Ishmael', stuck to my fingers and then to the carpet. Barnabas uses big sheets of drawing paper divided into squares, or even index cards. I could see why.

Maybe a simple list of the problems would be the place to start.

1. The manuscript – what is it?
2. Did Dr Fletcher's loss of interest come because of seeing the Telschi pictures? Or is there something coming out from the analyses he was having done? When will those results come?

3. Then what is this Teschi (crossed out) Telschi thing and how is it linked to GS etc?
4. Was it IP who phoned GS and if so why? *I know it was because he admitted it only I don't believe anything he says.*
   If so what did he say that made GS change his plans?

This didn't actually seem to be going anywhere, and I knew there were a lot more elements that I ought to bring in. I threw the pink pad down on the floor and watched Mr Spock stalk it and give it a pat, trying to encourage it to run away and be chased and killed.

The phone rang.

'Ah, Dido, you're upstairs.' My father's voice. He must have been trying the phone in the shop. 'Are you all right now?'

'A bit down,' I admitted. 'I can't see how . . .'

'How?'

'To get out of this mess.'

I could hear his snort. '*You* are *not* in a mess.'

'I am in a bewildered state,' I corrected myself in a spirit of cooperation. 'And I don't know how to get out of it.'

'I think I'll come over,' he said. And he arrived so quickly that I knew he must have taken a taxi. Perhaps he was also in a state of bewilderment.

He persuaded me that we had a shop which was meant to be open, and we went downstairs. The post hadn't arrived yet, which left us free to settle at the desk, turn the computer on, and discuss the situation.

'What happens,' Barnabas wondered suddenly, 'if one were to do an internet search for Telschi?'

The way to find out was to try it, and what did happen was that the screen enquired whether I had meant to say Tedeschi, and then offered Telschi as an alternative spelling for a certain Lithuanian synagogue and one form of a more general Lithuanian place name. If they were relevant, I failed to see how. But there seemed to be many, many more addresses here, and after a couple of minutes the search led to thousands of possibilities. It was going to take hours to look at everything listed – even just everything in English: a lot of it wasn't. But we could see that people had been arguing about the nature of that manuscript for years. There was too much stuff here.

'We'll have to look at all this,' I told my father. 'Next job, as soon as the catalogue's ready.' Or maybe there was a short cut? 'Barnabas, do you think it would be possible to find out anything more from Dr Fletcher?'

'More what?'

'When we went to see him yesterday, he'd changed his mind so suddenly about the manuscript! One day it was valuable and the next day it was nothing – something he wanted to get out of his way as fast as possible. If he explained it, I didn't catch what he meant. I wonder if there's something here that would explain?'

'Mmm. I could try.'

'Take him and buy him a beer,' I suggested. 'Find out why he was almost going to throw us out of the library yesterday.'

'I will turn up there this afternoon, perhaps,' Barnabas said slowly. 'And show a disturbing persistence. Perhaps in the meantime I should do something here?'

'Proof-read the catalogue? I'll find the file for you. Check that the prices are correct, or at least not stupid.'

'And you?'

'I heard the mail arrive a couple of minutes ago. I'll open it and take care of anything urgent. Then I might go and buy some stamps. I'll do one or two other errands after Ernie gets here.'

The plan worked well, if you allowed for the fact that I was thinking of other things most of the time and occasionally coming to and finding that I had wandered out into the front of the shop and was looking out at the street for signs of trouble.

One of the letters contained an order. That gave me a legitimate excuse to wrap up the two volumes of Florence Hardy's *Life of Thomas Hardy* for posting and ask Barnabas to tell Ernie as soon as he came in that I would phone him here shortly. I caught a distinctly fishy look in his eye as

154

I was about to leave. I turned back impatiently to the window.

'Dido?'

'Yes?'

'When will you be back?'

'Maybe in an hour.'

'Do you know what you're doing?'

'What? What do you mean?'

He looked at me from under his eyebrows. 'It's been going on for several days now. You keep looking out at the street. Whenever you come back from somewhere, and also when you leave, you look up and down the road. Why? What's going on?'

'I do?' I asked. But when I thought about it, I recognized the picture.

'Is Ishmael Peters bothering you?'

'No,' I said. 'Well, partly. I think really it's something else. The private investigator who was watching the place for a few days – he's looking for Peters too.'

'What's this?'

I explained: the man who had come into the shop but not to buy a book, just to hang around. Talking to Laura Smiley about him and getting her to find out who he was and to warn them I had complained. Then speaking to the man myself.

'From what Sergeant Smiley said, I thought he was going to leave,' I explained, 'but he came back again the next day. He hasn't been around more recently, I don't think. But I keep wondering whether he's out there. He was hired to find Ishmael Peters.'

'Hired by whom?' Barnabas enquired.

I explained why I didn't know.

'But the situation is making you nervous.' Barnabas thought about it. 'Why don't you find out who their client is? Could you ask Sergeant Smiley again? Just for your peace of mind.'

'I could try,' I agreed. The idea of getting even one thing clarified was tempting. And there was a good reason for asking which I suspected Laura Smiley would understand.

155

I decided to take fifteen minutes to try it. But when I rang, her mobile phone was switched off and the switchboard operator at the station said she was out on police business. I left the number of my own mobile phone and went out.

Luckily, my MPV was up at the far end of the street, so I was able to get to it without being seen from the shop, and I took yesterday's route back up to Wembley because that seemed as good a place to start as anywhere. I even found a parking place outside a little local post office somewhere on the way and got rid of the parcel.

The house in Elsley Road looked less dismal this morning, though the intervals of watery sunlight did nothing to hide its flaking paint or the cracked mortar in the walls. I parked the car in front of the door this time and went to ring doorbells, starting with the bottom one. Because I was watching for it, I saw the curtains at the window beside me give a little twitch. I rang harder.

The man who answered the door had a well developed beer belly, but that was his only likeness to Peters, being ten years younger, a bit taller, and black-haired.

He looked at me and grunted something.

'You have a tenant who moved in here about a week ago,' I informed him. I made it a statement because I didn't want to get an automatic denial. 'An American. Which is his bell?'

'Four. First floor back.'

I said, 'Is he in?' and pressed button number four without waiting for his answer.

'Maybe. Dunno.'

He started to close the door in my face, but there was a movement in the upstairs hallway which made him shrug and retreat behind the first door along the passage. By the time it had closed, Ishmael Peters was visible in the shadows at the top of the unlit staircase. He looked bedraggled, and his sweatshirt had a stain down the front.

'Miss Hoare? I didn't know. You want to come up?'

*No, I didn't.* I said, 'I'll wait here while you get your coat. The car is just outside, we can sit in that to talk.' I made my point by stepping inside, shutting the door, and standing in front of it. He teetered back and forth on his heels, nodded,

156

and went away. For a few minutes I played with the idea that I was going to have to run upstairs and dig him out of some cupboard, but he came back warmly dressed and mouth firmly shut, and joined me. We went out, I unlocked the passenger door and politely showed him into the seat. If he tried to jump out, he would discover one of the uses of my childproof locks. Then I walked around and settled into the driver's seat beside him.

'What name are you using here?'

'Bush.'

The American president. Why not?

He said, 'How did you know I was here?'

'You were followed.'

'What?'

'By a friend of mine.'

'Not the—'

'No, not the police. As it happens, I haven't told them where you are. Yet.'

He looked at me sideways. 'Why not?'

'Because I wanted to see whether you'd be willing to tell me some things I need to know or whether – well, if you like, whether I was going to have to hand the problem over to them.'

'What problem?'

I had to try: that was why I'd come. 'I need information. I can probably find the answers another way, it might just take me a bit longer. When you phoned Gabriel Steen, the day he was killed, what did you tell him?'

He turned a carefully blank face my way and said, 'What makes you think I phoned him?'

I shut my eyes to project dramatic weariness. Then, because I wanted to watch him, I opened them as quickly as I could without spoiling the effect and sighed. 'Why won't you just stop wasting my time? You already *told* me it was you. Besides, I just heard the beginning of the call. I heard him say, "Ish—something" I crossed my fingers. 'Then he went outside to talk to you, so that was all I heard. I didn't know then what "Ish" was, but I do now, and anyway you confirmed that last time we talked.'

157

I am a pretty good liar. Usually I can't mislead my father, but I can fool lots of other people. I watched Peters trying to decide what he should do. If he was an especially good liar, I hadn't seen any proof of it yet.

'All right, it doesn't matter. I told him that somebody he was trying to avoid had turned up in Amsterdam, and they'd been asking me where he was.'

'And you told them.'

'I couldn't help it,' he snapped.

I did another eyebrow-raising. 'Couldn't?'

'Miss Hoare, these are not nice guys. They are the ones who burned my studio out just to – well, to make me shut up. I did warn you that you have to get rid of the manuscript fast. They won't stop at just bashing *me* around, you know. You're a woman. No offence, but you don't know anything about this kind of people. He's – they're pros.'

For some reason I started thinking of the detective who had been watching the bookshop. 'Can you give me any names?' I asked him.

'I'm not suicidal,' he said, and that forced, high giggle filled the car. Nerves.

'So you told them that Gabriel had it. You told them he was in London. Did you tell them which bookshops he was going to call at? Or where he was staying?'

He turned white. 'I didn't . . . didn't know it would do such damage.'

I felt like doing some wild giggling myself, because he was being so . . . dim. 'You aren't the only person in the world with a mobile phone. They phoned somebody here in London, did they, and told them to find Gabriel and kill him?'

'No!' After a moment he went on. 'I couldn't think straight. What happened. It was my fault. Everything. I know, I know!'

'Who killed Gabriel?'

'They did.'

'*Who?* They came to you, and then they, or their friends over here in London, found him just after he'd left me, and they killed him while they were trying to get the manuscript from him? They thought he still had it. Yes? Is that it?' I'd started yelling.

He twitched and stayed silent, but it looked to me like a confession.

I was breathing hard. 'Just tell me everything that you know about the manuscript. I need to know what it is and where it came from. And whether somebody stole it.'

He clamped his mouth shut and shook his head. But I believed I'd got a part of the answer, even though it had been painful getting there. But the story still wasn't anything like complete. I felt like pushing him and his pitiful whining out of the car, but there was one last thing I ought to try first.

'The police are looking for you. Not the Essex police: I'm talking about a couple of detectives at New Scotland Yard from the section that specialize in crimes relating to art and antiquities. They came around to the shop after the Islington people told them you were staying at the Nayland.'

He jumped. 'What? They came to you? What did they say?'

'That they were looking for you.'

'That's all?'

'Yes.'

'Oh.' He thought about it for a minute, scowled, shook his head. 'I don't understand. Have you told them I'm staying here?'

I hesitated and then told him the truth. 'I think that I might have to. You understand?'

He said, 'I guess so,' slumping in his seat.

'So you'll be moving? Well, it isn't such a great place. Are you going to stay in London?' He nodded. 'You'll be able to find lots of other places just as good as this one.'

He looked drained, and I realized that I might start feeling sorry for Ishmael Peters. I can be such an idiot.

I pulled myself together. 'There's another possibility. You work out what you're going to do about all this and phone me at the shop as soon as you've decided. If there's anything you can tell the police about – well, about Gabriel, I could pass it on. Just stop making those stupid silent phone calls to me, and don't come back to the shop again. There's a detective keeping an eye on the place.' I didn't have to specify

a private investigator – let him think what he wanted to.
'Also there's something else you might think about.'

He scowled at me.

'When you're ready to talk to them yourself, you could always phone me and just ask for their names. The police. If you really haven't done anything wrong, you might be able to get out of a lot of trouble by going to them voluntarily.'

'I don't know what you're talking about, Miss Hoare. And what am I supposed to have done that they care about? And what silent phone calls are you talking about?' He started yanking at the door handle. I got out to open the door for him and watch him walk up the path and back into the crumbling house. For some reason, this interview had left me wiped out. And in the mood to kick somebody's ankle, especially his. This man was such a habitual liar that I doubted he would even know what was true and what wasn't. He would take the prize for being the most annoying person I'd ever met.

# Confessions

When I got back to the shop, I found that Ernie had arrived and Barnabas had gone out to lunch. Both things suited me nicely.

'Did my father say when he'd get back?'

Ernie shook his head vaguely, busy adjusting some text for the catalogue. He had found a couple of digitized images we'd made for a previous one, and we got out the camera and spent twenty minutes getting half a dozen more. One of them would make a good cover image: I'd get him to design that next. When I stopped to think about it, Ernie was almost a professional. When he finished his course in June, he would be earning a living doing just this, full-time, for somebody. It was a worry. I'd got used to depending on him in all kinds of ways.

I waited until he had finished trying out three slightly different ways of wrapping some text around a picture.

'Did he say where he was going?'

'British Library.'

Back to see Fletcher? Maybe Barnabas had found something that he wanted to talk over with the expert.

'And somebody phoned you,' Ernie added vaguely. 'That Sergeant Smiley. The professor phoned her this morning. He was talking to her about that detective in the car, and he asked her to phone somebody.' For some reason, my heart sank. Maybe it was just that I was going through a bad patch when most surprises turned out to be unwelcome ones. 'And then she called back after he left and said she had, and would you phone her when you have a moment. She says you know the number.'

Slowly I reached for the phone.

But when I got through to her, Sergeant Smiley's voice was lively.

I started by trying to apologize.

She laughed. 'Your father doesn't stand for any nonsense, does he? Look, don't worry. He told me that the investigator came back after I'd spoken to them, and he thought it was really starting to worry you. I phoned them again half an hour ago. The news is that their client has called off the job. So whatever was going on, it's finished now and you won't see them again.'

Still feeling a bit embarrassed, I thanked her for rescuing me. But I couldn't just leave it: I asked her, 'Did they say who the client was?'

'Some American insurance company I'd never heard of. Wait a minute, I made a note . . . It's called Tylor Insurance. Unless *you've* had some dealings with them, I'd guess that they're looking for Mr Peters because they have some money for him. He's an American citizen, after all, and it could be a pay-out from an old savings policy or something like that. All right?'

'All right,' I agreed. 'And thanks, I'll tell my father not to hassle you any more.'

She laughed and said goodbye, and I hung up and immediately started to wonder whether it was that easy. I gave myself a mental shake and turned to business.

So we worked. Ernie did things with the computer, and I stuck a sign on the street door which said 'Caution Wet Floor' and then mopped hard and tried to stop thinking about anything except the effects of the last few wet days on the cleanliness of our shop.

The phone was ringing in the office. Ernie answered it and beckoned to me through the office door, hissing, 'The professor.'

I wiped a wet hand on the leg of my jeans, went and took the receiver from him and said, 'Hello.'

'What's wrong?'

'I'm washing the floor. Where are you?'

'Still at the British Library, but we are about to go over to Rocca's for lunch. Dido, there is some news. We would be happy for you to join us. Dress nicely. Shall we say one fifteen?'

162

# Lasagne and Lecture

Rocca's is my father's favourite restaurant: Italian, family-run, and conveniently situated in Bloomsbury. It is a place we often go to for celebration or consolation. It certainly beat washing floors. Besides, Barnabas was up to something, and if Dr Fletcher was talking to us again I wanted to hear what he had to say. I emptied the bucket into the sink in the office, told Ernie to put up the 'Ring for Attention' sign and lock the door, in the hope that if trouble did turn up he would be able to identify it before he let it in, and to expect me back well before five o'clock. And fled.

They were already at one of the tables toward the back, near the kitchen, when I arrived. Old Mr Rocca was leaning over them and pointing to things on the menu. Barnabas was nodding. So was Dr Fletcher, whose smile seemed more genuine today. It is a comfortable restaurant. I joined them, sat myself down on the chair which Mr Rocca pulled out for me, and tried to relax.

'Order first,' Barnabas said as soon as I opened my mouth.

I said I'd have the salade niçoise and a glass of white wine. That done, I asked them how they were. They nodded at me in unison and asked how I was.

Presumably Barnabas noticed something from my expression. 'We have been talking over this whole business,' he offered.

Dr Fletcher nodded his agreement. It was starting to look like a twin-brothers act.

'About the similarities and the obvious relationship between the Telschi and the manuscript in our hands,' Barnabas amplified. 'Ernie showed me all the material that Dr Fletcher received from America. I don't suppose that

163

you've looked at it properly? There are extensive and surprising similarities between the two, enough for them to have come from the same hand. Some of the material appears to be identical.'

'So Dr Fletcher was worried –' I chose that word carefully – 'that ours is stolen?'

Barnabas sighed and shook his head. 'No. Dr Fletcher is clear that ours is a forgery.'

Fletcher nodded. 'I'm sorry, I couldn't think what to say to you. And I was even on the wrong track at that point. You see, we all know about the smuggling of antiquities into the USA over the past century. When I asked my friend in New Haven about this . . . yours . . . you know, he sent me the material I showed you so that I could compare the two. Then a few hours later I received an e-mail from somebody on an internet discussion group which is run from a college in the midwest. One of the members had been asking about your codex. I say a college site, and there are academics and museum curators on it, but at least one of them, a man called Doherty, is a policeman who works in this area. He advised me not to become too friendly with you.'

'Oh,' I said. It almost explained some things, provided you could really believe that Barnabas and I had been members of a notorious smuggling ring for the past century. Or had I misunderstood?

'I was able to suggest,' Barnabas put in rather drily, 'that Dr Fletcher should telephone Oxford and speak to the Provost of Queen's. I was given an impeccable character reference, I believe.'

Dr Fletcher mumbled something about being so sorry, about having to avoid getting involved in anything questionable because of his position. I did understand that he was only trying to protect his professional reputation, although his face had turned a deep red. At that point their plates of fettucini and my salad arrived, and we made ourselves busy eating until he had recovered.

'There's something else,' Fletcher said eventually. He looked from Barnabas to me. 'The ink. Did Professor Hoare tell you?'

'You were getting it tested.'

He cleared his throat. 'The results came back this morning, and it is very bad news. These inks leech into the vellum on which they are used, and . . . and . . .'

Barnabas interrupted. 'The Vinland Map, of course.'

Fletcher said simply, 'Yes.'

Even I knew about the Vinland Map, at least in general terms, because people have been arguing about it for nearly half a century. It is a map which shows the shores of Europe and a big island called Vinland far out in the Atlantic, which you would probably recognize as Greenland. If the map is real, then it shows that America was known to the Europeans well before Columbus landed there.

'It's the same problem,' Fletcher explained. 'When people made a chemical analysis of the ink, they found that it contained something called anatase, titanium dioxide, which has been used as a synthetic pigment only since the nineteen-twenties. The ink in the Vinland Map had yellowed so that it looked authentic, but the anatase seems to prove that it is a modern fake. There's been a tremendous argument about the whole thing, and only a couple of years ago a scholar used spectroscopy to examine ink-decay stains, which proved that although it looked like decaying iron-based ink, what had been used was carbon-based. There should have been no stains. And essentially, the ink on your manuscript is . . . Well, there's an argument about it . . .'

Barnabas inserted, 'Naturally.'

'But most people would say that the type of ink used is modern.'

'We have been thinking along similar lines,' Barnabas said a few forkfuls later. 'This morning I suddenly remembered something: spectral analysis. No, no, of course, you wouldn't have heard of it, Dido. It is a method which can be used in the decryption of certain types of cyphers by looking at the numerical distribution of characters in a document.' He looked at me out of the corner of his eye. 'To put it simply: what is the most commonly used letter in the English language? "E", of course. Now, obviously you can extend this. In English, again, how many occurrences of the letter "x" would you expect to find in comparison with "a"? Precisely. Provided you have a large enough sample, you can simply compare the distribution and placing of the characters in two different texts and determine whether those texts are, statistically speaking, in the same language.'

We were both staring at him. Dr Fletcher's jaw had dropped.

'You understand what needs to be done.'

As a matter of fact, I did; I have the advantage of knowing my father's ways of working.

I said, 'You could use this statistical method to examine the language used in our codex and compare it with long texts from various European languages, and . . .'

At the same time Dr Fletcher was objecting that this would require the use of a whole internet's worth of computer power.

'No, no, no.' Barnabas sighed. 'You are both missing the point. As it is a cipher, we would not expect the distribution to match a known language. The best evidence suggests that the Telschi manuscript is written in a cipher which has been created using a variant of the Cardan grille method. That is, a series of cards with holes cut in them is laid over a table of characters. This, by the way, was a favoured method of John Dee, the spy master to Queen Elizabeth the First. You understand where I am going with this?'

As a matter of fact, I thought I did. Maybe. 'You mean that the text of Gabriel Steen's codex and this other one in America should be compared by that means?'

Barnabas smiled approvingly. 'While we would be no further ahead in being able to *read* them, we would be able to ascertain how great a chance there is that both were made using the same grille.'

I thought of asking how long this would take and whether Dr Fletcher would be able to get it done. I thought not. Yet if we were taking it seriously, with a view to selling the thing for hundreds of thousands of pounds, would it be possible without?

'It is a forgery,' I said flatly.

The men looked at me and chorused, 'Probably.'

But if that were true . . . 'So then why was Gabriel Steen killed?' I asked.

They both stared at me.

Barnabas finally spoke. 'Because he knew about the nature of the codes and somebody wanted to keep him quiet . . . Because he was doing something against their instructions . . . Because they were trying to get the codex from him to sell it.'

'Ishmael Peters keeps saying that it's his fault.' It seemed that I had just lost my appetite.

Once again, Dr Fletcher was looking increasingly unhappy. He pulled himself together long enough to say, 'If there's anything I can do to help . . . ?'

I just shook my head.

My mobile rang while we were waiting for the bill. I'd forgotten that I'd left it on and had to look for it deep in my shoulder bag when I realized what the sound was. It had to be Ernie. I was panicking by the time I found it and answered with a subdued shriek.

But his voice was calm. 'Dido? You know that book you was telling me about the other day? *The Tel . . .*' He struggled with the pronunciation. '*Telssi Conspiracy*? I found it. It's in Ruebotham's list this month. Hardback, doesn't sound in good condition, and they want £10 for it . . .'

I said, 'Ernie, you're fabulous. Listen to me: phone them, say that we want it . . . tell him I want it urgently and ask him to send it special delivery. All right?'

He said, 'All right,' and hung up.

Barnabas was looking at me with mild curiosity, but that was enough to make me think. Maybe the Provost had assured Dr Fletcher of my father's probity, but I didn't think that we had received any similar assurances about him. I was mildly disturbed to realize what was going on in my head. A dead man once told me to trust nobody. It seemed like good advice right now.

'Just Ernie,' I told Barnabas calmly. 'He's located a book that somebody was asking about.'

Barnabas threw me a piercing look but went along with it. We'd all be taking a bus together up as far as the Euston Road, and when Dr Fletcher left us there, that would be the time for me to confess all.

# The Telschi

B en got to nursery school a little early next morning, and
by car, because I didn't want to risk missing my parcel
delivery. Naturally, the only parking bay that was empty by
the time I got back was at the far end of the street. I noticed
sourly as I jogged back that the convenient spot opposite the
shop, which I had left only fifteen minutes before, had been
grabbed by another strange car which wasn't displaying a
residents' permit. I ran across the road and was relieved not
to see a failed-delivery card waiting for me. So I let myself
in and went to see whether there was anything interesting
waiting on the answering machine. Two messages: one the
offer of a book, the other a greeting from my older sister,
Pat, telling me that one of my nephews had done really well
in his mock exams and asking me to phone her so she could
tell me all about it. It was another reminder that I was
supposed to have phoned her days ago. It felt like a message
from Mars, though it was really only from what most people
would call 'real life'.

I decided to buy the book, more for something to do than
for any other reason. Once I had sent off an e-mail to the
caller, I sat twiddling my thumbs.

Barnabas and the Post Office van arrived simultan-
eously. He brought the little parcel in and hung over me
while I dealt with packing tape and bubble wrap. Then I
handed it over to him and tried to find something to do
other than hang over his shoulder. Talking about bubble
wrap, were we running short? I went to investigate. And
printer ink?

Eventually Barnabas snapped, 'What about making some
coffee?'

168

'What about the book?'

He said, 'You'd better look for yourself.'

*The Telschi Conspiracy* was a normal-looking octavo in a grubby and faded green binding, with a loose frontispiece. I noted the pages of notes and bibliography at the end; if this didn't answer all our questions, it suggested that there were hundreds of other possibilities to explore.

I started by looking at the illustrations.

The style of draughtsmanship in the Telschi was awfully like that of our manuscript. I would have said, if anybody had asked me before everything had become so odd, that both codices dated from the same period and maybe the same source. I could almost see two monks sitting side by side in a mediaeval scriptorium, beavering away. Two or three of the pictures that were reproduced could have been copies of what we had, but others were unfamiliar, and I couldn't match them to any of our digital photographs. In both cases the pictures and text were mixed together. And the script, whatever it was: maybe an expert in mediaeval studies could have seen some differences, but it all looked the same to me. I asked Barnabas what he thought.

'I think,' he told me ponderously, 'that I should like to read this book before I commit myself. Will you be all right if I go upstairs and do just that? Phone me if anything comes up.'

'Why "conspiracy"?'

'Precisely,' he said and took himself and the book away.

I spent the time making work in the shop. Most of it consisted of checking catalogue entries. Eventually I went upstairs, made a couple of sandwiches, delivered one to Barnabas, whom I found in the sitting room with the book, scribbling notes as he read, and took mine downstairs. A few people drifted in and out and even spent a few pounds.

In the middle of the afternoon the phone rang. When I answered it, nobody was there.

That reminded me about the Peters problem, and about the decision I was supposed to have made already. I'd given him a day – more than twenty-four hours – to contact me.

He knew I was here, yet he wasn't . . . no, I could probably say he was actually *refusing* to speak to me. Or the police.

I rang Chris Kennedy's number and was told by his voicemail that he was out. After a little more thought I tried Laura Smiley's mobile and got a human voice. I could hear people talking in the background. She was busy with something, so I came straight out with it.

'I found Ishmael Peters. I asked him to contact the police, but I don't suppose that he has.' When I'd finished telling her everything, I could almost see her shaking her head at me.

'He told you a fairy tale,' she suggested. 'Well, it doesn't matter. I think I'd better get on to the people at SO1. They'll be in touch with you.'

I couldn't stop myself from trying one last time. 'Do you know why they're interested in him?'

She answered without hesitation: 'I know that it's an old case. Something about the illegal export of art works. I understand that anything over a certain age and value sold abroad from an EU country requires an export license, and that the regulations are sometimes ignored. I don't know much about this myself, because it's handled centrally, but probably there's a lot of money involved.'

I did know some of the details myself. I said slowly, 'I suppose I should talk to them.'

'You aren't . . .'

'Aren't what?' I asked her, but my heart was sinking. 'Involved? Of course not!'

'But Ishmael Peters is?'

'He might be,' I agreed carefully. 'I have no idea, but it would make sense. I suppose I could phone those men . . .'

'I'm going to,' she said. 'Don't worry. I'll get them to contact you. Listen, Ms Hoare, would you tell your father that I was able to do what he asked?'

I struggled for a moment, then remembered what Ernie had told me. 'He phoned you yesterday about the private investigator, didn't he? I'm sorry —'

'Oh, don't worry. It sounded to me as though they were being a little too pushy, frankly. But you won't see them again. It took them a little while to contact their client, but the job has definitely been called off now. And I'd better go. Get back to me if there are any more problems. Good luck!'

I thanked her for her help and hung up, wondering why I was likely to need good luck and what was making me feel so guilty. Should I ask Leonard Stockton to bring the manuscript around and accompany me while I handed it over to SO1 and tried not to get arrested? Maybe. But not until I could work out where an Arts and Antiquities investigation into illegally exported works could possibly fit into this situation. That just didn't make sense.

# Saturday Business

When the alarm went off on Saturday morning, my first impulse was to throw the clock across the bedroom, but I was awake enough to remember that this might frighten Ben. I fumbled blindly and switched it off. Then I heard the toilet flush and the pad of bare feet, and felt somebody leaning against my bed to look for signs of life.

'G'morning,' I whispered, and forced my eyes open. Mr Spock arrived and leaped to join us. Right, but I still wasn't looking forward to the day.

The phone rang in the sitting room just before nine o'clock. I waited for the answering machine to switch on so I could make sure who was calling. A familiar voice said, 'Dido? I just wanted—'

I grabbed the receiver. 'I'm here. Chris, hello? What is it?'

A short silence made me realize that my voice had betrayed some of the stress I was feeling.

'Not much. Remember I promised to talk to my contact in Amsterdam again?'

'Yes?'

'Well, I got something on Gabriel Steen, though it's not much. He's been living in Amsterdam for the past few years, and he dealt in second-hand books at a low level. There's nothing against him on the record. They know more about Ishmael Peters. He's a minor American artist, a painter who exhibits when he gets the chance and sells prints and water-colours through a website. He's been in Amsterdam for almost twenty years, and his place of business was recently destroyed by arson. You know all this. I asked my contact whether there was any suggestion that he had set the fire himself for the insurance, and the answer to that seems to be no. Apparently he was insured for a small amount – no reason to risk jail for a few thousand euros. He has no convictions except a twelve-year-old suspended sentence for selling somebody a Van Gogh drawing which was a forgery. His defence was ignorance – he told them he just didn't realize there was anything wrong with it. And he agreed to turn and give evidence against his co-defendant. That was a known forger – a French citizen called Renaud, who got a prison sentence, so maybe Peters was lucky. The only interesting thing is that nobody knows where he is at the moment. But you knew that too.' *I did*. 'Has he been in touch again?'

'Sort of. Ernie found out where he's been living, and I talked to him. The Art and Antiquities people at Scotland Yard are looking for him too. And an American insurance company, though they seem to have given up now.'

'What?'

'Apparently. They hired a London investigation agency to find him by watching the shop. Laura Smiley found out about it for me.'

'What insurance company?' His tone was incredulous.

'They're called Tylor Insurance.'

'Never heard of them. Are they real?'

I told him I'd never heard of them either.

'I'll see if I can find out anything. Dido, what about your mad American?'

'Oh, Peters, Peters – SO1 were asking me about him, they didn't say why, and I told him that he should talk to them, but he hasn't, and now he's left the place where he was staying. I thought I had to tell them I'd spoken to him, but now I wish I hadn't. They're going to make a fuss about my not calling 999 about two days ago.'

'Tell them you will, next time.' He wasn't actually laughing out loud. 'I don't suppose he'll just disappear in a puff of smoke and leave you alone now?'

'Not while I've got Gabriel Steen's codex,' I said sourly. 'And there've been signs that he's keeping an eye on the shop, hanging around. I've been having some silent phone calls. Sometimes he admits that he's doing it and sometimes he looks all wide-eyed when I accuse him. The next time he comes visiting, I swear I'm going to kick him where it hurts.'

'That's only fair,' he said gravely. 'If you need backup, phone me and I'll help with the kicking. Look, it was one of those nights at work. I'm going to get some sleep, but my mobile will be on.'

I hung up and the phone rang.

'Dido? Good morning, how is everything there?'

'Fine,' I told Barnabas as cheerfully as I could manage. 'You?'

'Pat has been phoning me. I told her that you were intolerably busy but would speak to her before the day is out. I shall be leaving for there in a few minutes. Should I bring anything?'

'Just yourself. I'm expecting the police some time today, so it would be good to have somebody here for Ben.'

'They will be arresting you?' my father enquired acidly.

I said that I really didn't think so, but he promised me he would hurry anyway.

When Ben and I got downstairs after breakfast, we found that the post had arrived early – probably the postman wanted to get home in time to watch the football. I settled Ben in the office and talked to him about the meaning of life while I was going through the motions of getting ready for the business day and thinking about Gabriel Steen and Ishmael Peters. I unlocked the door at ten, and Ernie arrived at top speed twenty minutes later, only just before Barnabas, who arrived early carrying his old briefcase. And then some customers started to come in. Three of them bought books. By the time that the last one had left and somebody else had arrived, things seemed to be looking up.

Ten minutes later, Ernie, who happened to be looking past me toward the door, said, 'Trouble.'

I jumped guiltily and turned. Alan Quinn stopped in the open doorway and looked around. He nodded at me, considered the situation, raised his eyebrows and beckoned: could I come outside? I nodded to him and told Barnabas I'd be back in a minute; then I joined him on the pavement.

174

'I've got something I want you to look at,' he said without preamble. 'We ought to go upstairs, if you don't mind.' That was the point when I noticed his driver getting out of an anonymous grey car parked a little way up the street. He opened the back door of the car, pulled out a grey box and came to join us.

I said, 'Of course. Though I ought to warn you that my father will come up in about two minutes.'

Quinn laughed. 'We'd better get on with it, then.'

In the sitting room, he placed the box gently on the coffee table and opened flaps at the top and side, revealing what looked like a slightly melted oval-shaped lump of plastic. 'Look at it as long as you need to, but don't touch. Do you know what it is?'

I seemed to, but I went on staring for long enough to be absolutely sure. It had obviously been in a fire, and the bright blue and white of Gabriel Steen's cycling helmet had melted and distorted, the colours darkened and the smooth surface matted and dulled.

'Yes. That's the one he was wearing when he rode off. I mean, it looks the same. What happened to it?'

'There was a burnt-out car in a field off a minor road outside Billericay. It was reported days ago, but nobody could get around to doing anything about it for a while. You get a lot of those, and you deal with them as and when there isn't anything more urgent, you understand, because it's usually kids joy-riding. When they finally got to this one, they checked the number plates and found that it wasn't your usual rusting wreck, but something a car-hire firm had reported stolen from their lot in Harwich. The damage wasn't too bad – I think that the tank must have been fairly low – and when they had a look inside they found this thing in the boot. I'm getting the forensic people to go through the whole interior properly, but so far they haven't found anything else. But I remembered what you said. My idea is that Steen's body and bicycle were carried in the car to the place where they were found, and after they'd dumped them his killers got rid of the car and tried to destroy any traces they might have left.

I told him carefully that I would swear that this looked exactly like the helmet Gabriel was wearing the last time I saw him. I was still curious. 'Why would they steal a car from a hire car lot?'

'Good question.' He had relaxed a little, now that he had got an answer, and was carefully doing up the container. 'Possibly they thought it wouldn't be missed as quickly as somebody's personal vehicle.'

I could understand that, when I thought about it, but on the other hand . . . 'You don't think it was taken by somebody who hired another car from them at about the same time?'

He stopped what he was doing to look at me. 'As a matter of fact, we are checking that possibility . . . Miss Hoare.'

'I have a criminal mind,' I told him and was glad to see that he could laugh, though I noticed the other man giving me a look.

The door downstairs opened and closed noisily, and we could all hear the footsteps on the stairs. Quinn slid the last flap into place and straightened up just as Barnabas joined us.

'Dido?'

'I'm coming.'

'Saturday,' my father explained to the policemen, 'is one of our busiest days.'

'We were just leaving,' Quinn said.

I caught the ghost of wink. Sharp man. Maybe he had a father – or a superintendent – a bit like Barnabas.

# The Real Business

It was almost noon when the car drew up outside on a yellow line and one of the Scotland Yard men appeared – the taller one with the blond hair. I tried to remember his name. Page, that was it. He came in and looked around, and I squared my shoulders and went to join him.

'DS Smiley rang us yesterday. You've seen Mr Ishmael Peters?'

I'd been through it all with her, but now we did it again.

He asked a few questions, but he wasn't taking note of my answers. In fact, he looked bored by the whole business. He had heard the story already, just as I had told it already, and I thought that we were probably both getting fed up with Peters and all his deeds.

'I wonder why he's still hanging around? Look, Miss Hoare, we're not sure why he's avoiding us. We aren't going to charge him, we just want to talk to him. We need some information. It could all be friendly if he'd just cooperate. Will you tell him that?'

'I can tell him, but he won't believe anything I say.'

'The man is either stupid or . . .' He bit the comment off in mid-sentence. Presumably he'd been going to say something like 'mad as a hatter' but decided not to speak improperly. Policemen are impartial, aren't they?

I went and sold some books. There was something unreal about business today, as though Gabriel and Ishmael Peters and the codex which was almost certainly a forgery were more real than anything else, instead of being just a distraction. At some point when I was passing through the office, wrapping a book and taking a credit card payment for it, I found myself saying to Ernie, 'Tylor Insurance.'

Not surprisingly, he looked blank.

'See if you can find out anything about a company called Tylor Insurance. It's American.'

By the time I had completed the sale, he was beckoning me over to the desk.

'Look,' he said. 'Is this it?' He had called up the home-page of the Tylor Insurance Company, based in Tylor, Texas, offering auto insurance and a few related products.

'Is it the only one? I don't see how this can be right.'

'The only one I can see,' Ernie said.

Maybe I had misheard the name. I gave up – there were too many other things that needed my attention.

By five o'clock, things were quietening down.

I don't know how long the car had been parked right in front of the shop – on Saturday afternoons the streets around are crowded with shoppers' cars constantly coming and parking and going away again. Because I happened to be facing the window at the moment, I did see its doors open and two men emerge, and I also noticed – and marvelled – that they didn't stop to lock up before they crossed the pavement. However one of them, the driver, stopped, turned around, and stood on guard, facing the car with his back to the display window. The other one came in.

I had never seen him before. He was a tall man in his forties, with dark, tidy hair and pale eyes in a tanned face. He wore a dark grey short coat that somehow managed to look very expensive although it was absolutely plain, and underneath it a slightly lighter pinstripe suit, well pressed.

Curious, I nodded a greeting and finished replacing a couple of books on a shelf and checking on the other customers, who all seemed to be contented.

He was at my elbow. 'Are you Miss Hoare?' It was an American drawl. Southern.

I looked up at him, still trying to work out what was going on. He held out his business card. It was very plain – black letters on white, just the names, himself and the company for which he worked: Richard Tipton, the Tylor Insurance Company of Tylor, Texas.

I did the only thing possible: managed to find just enough breath to mumble, 'How do you do?'

'Thank you,' he said. 'I'm interested in a manuscript book that you have. A man called Ishmael Peters' – the pale eyes seemed to flicker – 'told my client that you have a mediaeval manuscript for sale. May I see it?'

I heard myself say, 'I'm sorry, no. It's not here any more.'

He said quietly, 'I assure you I'm willing and able to pay a fair price.'

If I'd known in advance, I would have thought everything out. Since I hadn't, I did the easiest thing and fell back on a kind of truth. 'You see, I sent it out on approval to somebody a few days ago, but they phoned me yesterday afternoon. They say it's a modern forgery. I'm sorry.'

'Really? Well, well.' He frowned slightly. 'That's a blow. Are you . . . Is this customer sure? I'd still be interested in seeing it. Even if he's right, those kind of things can be very interesting. Where is it now?'

'He's sending it back. I suppose it'll arrive on Monday or Tuesday.'

'I'll come by on Monday just in case.'

'We're not open on Mondays,' I said, 'and anyway it may not get here by then. I'm fed up of all this.'

'I might still be interested,' he said slowly, 'in buying it.'

'It's a forgery,' I repeated flatly. 'Somebody told me that, and it seems to be true. You want to buy a forgery?'

He said, 'I think I know the item. I could make you an offer.'

I let him see me looking very puzzled and thinking about it. After a few moments I decided to look less glum and very greedy. I widened my eyes at him. 'You do understand it might not be old? Twentieth century. If that's understood, would you like to make me an offer? Let's say a provisional offer, of course, until you can look at it. What kind of sum were you thinking of?'

I was trying to give him the wrong idea about me, and apparently I was doing pretty well. He looked at me silently with those pale eyes and finally said, 'It could be worth fifteen thousand dollars to me.'

I said flatly, 'Oh . . . Well, I'm not sure . . .'

'I might be able to go a little higher.'

'I was thinking about twenty.'

'That might be possible. We can talk about it when I see it.'

I shrugged. 'Well, if you're in the neighbourhood, and you want to drop by on the off-chance at about two o'clock on Monday, I could come in specially to let you have a look at it then. Or, better still, if you tell me where I can contact you, I could let you know when it does get here.'

'I'm touring. What do you say I phone you here at two on Monday?'

'I'll give you our card,' I said, trying to project eagerness with more of that ignorant greed.

'It's OK, Miss Hoare, I've got your number.' He nodded. 'Goodbye then.'

I couldn't have said another word. I tried to smile, but I think that I nodded like an idiot instead. Then I stood and watched him slowly leaving the shop. It seemed to me as though he was moving underwater.

The second man snapped to attention when Tipton appeared. The two of them exchanged a word and then moved over to the car and climbed in. I waited for them to drive away. They were taking their time about it, but it couldn't really have been more than a minute before I saw the car start to move off. As it passed, I even had the time to see the hire car firm's big sticker in the rear window.

Then I turned around very carefully and had just enough time to totter into the office. I got as far as the waste-paper basket before I was sick. I was vaguely conscious of Ernie jumping up and asking whether I was all right, then rushing to push the office door shut. When I'd stopped vomiting, I sat down and put my head between my knees.

'I'll be all right,' I said from that position. 'Ernie, if you don't mind – please just take the waste-paper basket outside and throw it away.'

He disappeared, holding it at arm's length. In a couple of minutes, he was back with Barnabas, who brought the half-empty bottle of Irish whiskey that I keep upstairs for him.

'Drink this,' he commanded, and handed me a huge slug in one of the coffee mugs. I wasn't so sure about that, but I took a sip. Half an ounce afterwards, I got myself off the floor and into a chair. Ernie had gone out to mind the shop, and Barnabas was getting angry and saying, 'Dido, what happened? Kindly just tell me. Right now!'

I said, 'I panicked for a minute.' And I told him about the hire firm's sticker I'd seen on the car.

'Would you like some more whiskey?' he asked quietly when I'd finished.

'Probably not on an empty stomach.'

'This must stop!' he exploded.

'That's a good idea,' I said.

'Well, what are you going to do about it?'

I said, 'I'm thinking.'

After a while, he snorted and took the bottle away with him.

At a quarter to six, the phone rang, and I answered it.

Barnabas's voice said, 'We are waiting for you. Ben is getting hungry, and I want to talk to you about this afternoon. And also the book you gave me. I've finished it. Fascinating stuff. I hadn't realized. Can you leave Ernie to close up?'

The place was empty, and it was only business; we were supposed to shut at six anyway.

I said, 'Coming. I just have to pay Ernie and check things. Give me ten minutes.'

# Sunday Trading

By eleven o'clock next morning, Barnabas and Ben had removed themselves until supper time and I was about to descend to the shop and open up. There was quite a lot of business to take care of. Most of it was necessary though likely to be unprofitable.

I started by phoning Laura Smiley on her mobile. When she answered, I gave her my name and started to apologize for interrupting her weekend.

'Don't worry,' she said. 'I'm on duty this weekend anyway. You've just interrupted me puzzling about an overnight break-in at a local church. Somebody stole an old slide projector. Is something wrong?'

'I think so. You remember about the Americans who hired David Martin to watch the shop? Well, somebody else has turned up from the United States. This is getting weirder and weirder.'

By the time that I'd finished telling my story, nothing seemed any clearer.

'So they're supposed to phone you tomorrow, but you think that they'll probably just come back?'

'Unless they turn up again today,' I said glumly. 'I don't know what they're up to. But I did say that the manuscript wouldn't be here until tomorrow, so I suppose today is safe enough.'

'Safe . . . Are you on your own there?'

'Barnabas and Ben are out for the day, but Ernie . . .' I was watching the street door as I talked to her, and so I was able to change the sentence to, 'Ernie has just got here.'

'All right. Listen, Ms Hoare, I have a meeting in ten

182

minutes, and then I need to make a few phone calls. But I'll be there before one o'clock. Will that be all right? There are things in your story that I don't understand, but maybe we can get something sorted out. If you start to feel uneasy about anything you see, just lock up and get out.'

I said, 'I can't evacuate forever, you know.'

'No. All right, then keep your eyes open and call me on this phone if anything happens: I'll keep it switched on. And I'll see you later.'

I noticed that having my worries taken seriously was somehow no great comfort. So I switched on a smile for Ernie and watched him get the computer running.

'We're a'most there,' he assured me brightly. 'You checked the last five or six pages? Then we can print a copy out and get it off to the printers. They open today?'

'We'll finish today and deliver it tomorrow first thing,' I announced. 'I got as far as the last couple of pages yesterday. Let me finish now. You take care of the shop until I've done it.'

I spoke into the jangle of the little Nepalese bells on the opening door. First customer. No, there were two of them. The more the merrier. Ernie went out to greet them, and I forced myself to concentrate, because there had been too many interruptions but it was all nearly finished at last. When I had finished checking the item about John Vassos's *Phobia*, an illustrated book on Art Deco from 1931, it took me a moment to realize that the job really was complete. A minute later and Ernie and I had changed places and I could hear the printer starting up as I took his place in the shop. Everything appeared pleasantly ordinary. I looked at my wristwatch.

The bells jangled again, I jumped, and Chris Kennedy came striding up the aisle.

He grabbed my arm and looked closely at my face. 'Day off,' he reminded me. 'Until four o'clock, anyway. Barnabas rang me. I have a bit of news for you, by the way. Are you all right? What happened?'

'Chris, an American turned up here yesterday. He wanted to see the codex, and maybe buy it. I told him it was a forgery, but he didn't seem to be put off. Do you remember I asked you about a Tylor Insurance company?'

'Tylor. I looked it up on the web, but I couldn't see anything special about it. Every town in Texas seems to have a little local insurance company of its own, named for the place and mostly selling car insurance.'

'Well, the man who came here yesterday was an employee of Tylor Insurance.'

Chris looked at me sharply. 'What! Why on earth . . . ?' I gave him a raised eyebrow copied from my father, and he laughed and shook his head. 'All right! What else? What's bothering you?'

'When they were driving away, I saw a car-hire firm's sticker in the back window.'

'Ye-e-es,' he said, and then, 'Oh, wait a minute. Yes, maybe you should contact Alan Quinn and tell him about it.'

I should probably have done it yesterday, if I'd been thinking straight. Maybe it didn't mean anything. Even so . . . At the weekend it might be easier for Laura Smiley to get hold of him, and she would be here in less than an hour.

Chris pottered around and looked at books. I also pottered and straightened up what was on the lower shelves. In the office, the printer stopped and started up again and then, a few minutes later, a whoop and a shout came from Ernie. When I reached the door, I expected to see flaming sheets of printer paper flying about the room. Instead, Ernie was looking up from the computer screen with a huge grin on his face.

'Dido, come an' look at this!'

I went and looked over his shoulder and found myself staring at a screen which showed a simple website with some now very familiar-looking illustrations on it, and a heading that read 'Telschi Manuscript Discussion Group'. Below it was a long list of message titles.

Ernie was beaming at me. 'When you asked me to look for that book, I found this place. It's a bulletin board about the Telssi manuscript. Lots of people talking about their theories. People from different universities and stuff. So I posted a small version of one of your pictures of a page of the manuscript just to see if anybody recognized it or anything. There's over six hundred replies! Everyone's talking about it! They're all arguing about what it is and how old and whether it's real, or what. Hey!'

I said, 'Oh.'

He looked at me anxiously. 'Do you mind?'

There was no simple answer. I told him to forget about it. Then I changed my mind. 'Ernie, have you read them all? All these posted messages?'

'Not yet! I only just realized.'

'Well,' I said, 'while you're overseeing the printing job, I'd like you to start. Don't bother about the ones that just say things like "Wow" or "Ooooooohhh it must be old", or things like that. But make a note of every message that's come from somebody who seems to know about this kind of manuscript and who is actually taking part in a serious discussion, right? Do you see what I mean?'

'Nerdy types.'

I agreed.

When I backed into the shop and closed the office door, Chris was hovering. 'What is it?'

I told him.

'So everybody in the world could know by now that you have this thing. Can they identify you? Ernie wasn't actually advertising, was he?'

I yanked the door open again and said, 'Ernie, is there any way that picture can be traced to here?'

There was a moment's thoughtful silence from inside the office.

'Well, it can't be linked direct to the shop. But the board records every poster's IP number, so I s'pose someone could do a reverse DS on it to finger our ISP and then compare it to a list of booksellers' e-mail addresses. Um. So if somebody really wanted . . .'

Chris shut his eyes briefly. He said, 'That's interesting.'

I just nodded and shut the door again and was still trying to think through the consequences of all this when the street door opened and Laura Smiley walked in. She looked hard at me.

'What's happened?'

'Oh,' I said, and struggled for words. What hadn't happened lately? I gave her a sketch of yesterday's visit.

When I mentioned the hire firm sticker on the car, she stopped me. 'Which firm?'

'Hertz.'

'Ah.'

'Ah?'

She didn't laugh. 'That's the firm whose car was stolen and torched.'

'Coincidence?'

'There *is* such a thing as coincidence,' she admitted, 'but it's not an explanation that you're supposed to accept very easily when you're in the middle of a murder investigation. I'm sorry, but I think something had better be done about this appointment you've set up for tomorrow. Maybe you should just stay closed and let them leave a message on your answering machine. In case they do come around, I probably ought to advise you to leave a note for them on the door saying that your manuscript didn't come back, and then lock everything up and stay out of the way.'

'When could I come back?'

'I know it's not a permanent answer, but it might give us a little more time to get everything sorted.'

I said, 'I don't need more time. I've already told him that the manuscript is a forgery, and tomorrow I intend sell it to him "with all faults".'

Chris said, 'What?'

I said, 'Why not? Unless somebody can work out why I shouldn't, why *not* do it? If it were real it would be different, because it would have a historical standing. If it isn't genuine, I can do anything I want to with it, and I will because when they've got what they want, they'll go away. They'll be out of my hair. Alan Quinn would probably like to arrest them for Gabriel Steen's murder, and if he has any evidence he can do just that. Maybe they'll relax and it will be easier for him to take them by surprise. It can't do any harm.'

'Then,' Smiley said slowly, 'somebody should be here with you tomorrow.'

'I'll see whether Ernie —'

'I don't mean Ernie,' she said. 'In fact, you tell him that you don't need him tomorrow.' Then she pulled out her phone.

But when I went in to give that message to Ernie, I found him too absorbed in something on the computer screen to listen. I went and looked over his shoulder. Somebody was talking about the frequency distributions being out of phase.

'I don't get this,' he said sadly. 'It's this guy at Oslo University. He keeps posting, but I don' know what he's talking about. He wants me to send him some more pages, though.'

I stopped for long enough to think it out as carefully as I could, given the speed with which things were starting to move. And came to a decision.

'Send another few pictures,' I said. 'Send the pages that are all writing. Never mind about the pictures right now. And Ernie, print out all the messages this person in Norway has posted, because Barnabas will want to see them. I think he might want to talk to this man.'

# Being Critical

When I got upstairs, Ben greeted me at the door with a finger held up to his lips. 'Shh! Grandpa's asleep.'

Grandpa's voice came from the sitting room saying, 'I am not asleep, I'm thinking.' He appeared suddenly in the doorway and added, 'I want to talk to you. Things are becoming . . .' He stopped, threw a quick glance at Ben, and finished, 'Critical.'

'What's "cri-ti-cal"?' Ben asked as I leaned down and gave him a hug.

'It means there's something very, very important that's just going to happen, and you have to try hard to think about it and decide what to do.'

'And also whether there is something wrong with the problem,' my father added. 'Dido, I have finished that book. Very thought-provoking. I haven't yet worked out why the Telschi manu—'

'Not now,' I suggested. 'It's supper time. Later?'

Barnabas shrugged, nodded, said, 'I'll be making a few notes,' and wandered back into the sitting room. Ben and I turned the other way and went into the kitchen, where Mr Spock was already waiting.

By the time I'd got Ben into bed, I just wanted to follow his example. Barnabas had other ideas.

'Having looked in your fridge a little while earlier,' he said, 'I took the liberty of phoning out for a pizza. You look tired. But we must try to get things sorted out, you know. Exactly what happened yesterday?'

'Somebody came in and asked about buying the codex. And when he left, I realized that he and the man with him were driving a hire car. Gabriel Steen's body was carried to where it was found in a stolen hire car, and I said to Inspector Quinn that maybe it was stolen by somebody who had hired another of their cars legitimately. It was a kind of joke, when I said it, but when I saw this one—'

'Wait a minute! How did this new man know about the codex?'

'He said that Ishmael Peters told his client about it, and his client sent him to get it. He had a business card – he works for a Texan insurance company.'

'An insurance . . . ? Never mind, we'll come back to that. What did he say when you told him it is a forgery?'

'That he would still be interested in buying it.'

'While we're at it, how do *you* know that it's a forgery?'

I understood exactly what Barnabas was getting at. 'I told the man that I'd offered it to somebody who has just turned it down as a fake, and that he's sending it back. This man who came here today, Tipton, is coming back on Monday to look at it. I told him to phone me at two o'clock, but I wouldn't count on him not just coming back then.'

Barnabas said, 'Ah,' and left it for the moment. 'Now, let's get back to the beginning.'

'Gabriel Steen . . .'

'No, Ishmael Peters. He's the beginning. He is an artist, and therefore the person who probably has the technical ability to create something like the codex. Remember also the Van Gogh forgery . . .' He consulted his notes. 'Twelve years ago.'

'He didn't do that, though. That was made by an old forger called . . .'

'Renaud. True. But Peters was involved. The old man's apprentice?'

'He testified against him.'

'To save his own skin, I presume. And it succeeded. I wonder what became of Monsieur Renaud. If he was an old man at the time of the trial, he may well have died since.' I could see him adding a tick and a question mark to his notes. 'Though on the other hand . . .'

I waited. While I was waiting, the bell rang and the pizza

arrived. We were distracted long enough for Barnabas to get a second wind.

'On the other hand, can we really believe that Peters is capable of making a codex without guidance? It must have been a complex task.'

'We don't know.'

'We don't know,' Barnabas repeated, nodding. 'Now then: on to stage two. Gabriel Steen turned up in London, probably for the first time in several years, bringing the codex with him. We assume he was intending to sell it, though not to us. He received a phone call from . . . ?'

'Peters wouldn't admit it for a while, but in the end he said that he phoned to tell Gabriel they were in trouble, and that he needed some money, as quickly as possible.'

'What kind of trouble?'

'Peters said that some people had traced him and were asking about the codex. He said they were dangerous, and that they forced him to tell them about Gabriel's trip, and that he couldn't help it. He was giving the impression that he'd been in terrible danger.'

Barnabas snorted. 'Does that suggest anything to you? He testified against his old mentor in order to avoid a jail sentence, and this time he betrayed Gabriel to save his own skin.'

'I'm not sure that follows.'

'Neither am I,' my father admitted briskly. 'There is a big gap between those possibilities and the facts that you actually witnessed.' He looked at me. 'How did they find him? Steen, I mean. They had to find him if they were going to murder him.'

'Ishmael?'

'The person who knew where he was, and who told him to drop everything and head straight back to Amsterdam? Mobile phone, just keeping in touch, where are you now?'

I looked at this picture for a moment. 'That's horrible. But Barnabas, he kept admitting that it was all his fault. He told me time and time again how nasty and violent and dangerous those men were. Suppose some of them stayed with him until they found Gabriel? And then Gabriel didn't have it after all. Maybe they tried the same tactics on him, to find out what he had done with the thing. But he was a stronger man than Peters, and they killed him without getting what they wanted. And they left Peters alone then, because . . . because he was their last link to the codex, they thought that he knew where the codex is and they'd only be able to get it, in the end, by watching him . . . No wonder he tried to disappear. It's not the police that he's hiding from.'

'Not a brave man.'

'No,' I agreed.

'He probably wouldn't really want to tell anyone this story.'

'No.'

'But what I still can't make out,' said Barnabas, a moment later, 'is why they are so anxious to get their hands on what does seem to be a modern forgery. I should explain to you about what I've been doing. There was enough. Enough in the *Conspiracy*.'

It had been a long day, and I wasn't in the mood for more codes or ciphers. 'Enough what in the what?'

'Enough of the *Telschi* in the book you gave me to read. That is, the real *Telschi*, or at least the previously known *Telschi*. Enough of the text was reproduced in the book to give a satisfactory sample for simple statistical analysis. Not – I grant you – enough to offer what I have discovered as proof, per se, rather than merely another strong indicator of what we already suspect. The frequency distributions do not match.'

'Unless they're out of phase.'

He looked at me, taken aback. My satisfaction was short lived, though, because when he asked me to explain I was only repeating what Ernie had said, and I hadn't really understood it then either. I did explain about Ernie's post on the internet and the six hundred replies, especially the ones from the researcher in Oslo who had been doing statistical comparisons of the page Ernie had posted there, and had been loudly demanding more samples in at least two dozen of those six hundred replies.

'Nevertheless,' Barnabas said after we had completed this

diversion, 'I still do not understand what Mr Peters thinks, or thought, he is doing. Or, for that matter, why your new customer would wish to buy it. Unless they thought that it might somehow be possible to take it to the United States and pass it off as the real thing? It seems unlikely. Twenty or thirty years ago, it might well have been possible, but now?

'For example, take the Vinland Map. When that appeared in 1965, it caused a tremendous stir because it seemed to provide evidence that Christopher Columbus was *not* the first European to discover America! Papers were published within months, then books. But if something like that were to appear nowadays, it would be all over the internet in a week. As indeed it is: you only have to look and you will see pictures of the map, with records, analyses, references . . . Some of them are very recent. Everybody in the developed world must have access. A second copy would be discredited immediately.

'So when something like our codex is discovered, you would expect the interest to be tremendous, as Ernie has already discovered, and it too would be immediately discredited, especially with such a dubious provenance. It would have some curiosity value, I presume, but only as an object, an article with some claim to interesting craftsmanship. And yet, and yet . . .'

I yawned and said, 'That was a good pizza.'

Barnabas said, 'You look exhausted. We need to talk more about your American, and what you will do on Monday. I believe that you should have the police in the shop when he arrives. Or in case he arrives.'

I'd had a few ideas about all that, but they would make more sense after a night's sleep. For the moment, I was more concerned about tomorrow.

Barnabas threw a piercing glance my way and said, 'We'll discuss it in the morning. I'll be here before nine.'

'And take Ben away before the shop opens,' I said. 'He ought to have an interesting day, not spend it hanging around.' I didn't add, 'and possibly be in danger', though it was in my mind.

192

At the last minute, my father stopped in the doorway and turned. 'When you wake up,' he said, 'I'd like you to think about something. Why does Ishmael Peters pretend he is still in danger? Steen had the codex, and it wouldn't be hard to understand if somebody were trying to steal it from him. Peters does *not* have the codex and hasn't had it for some time, and everybody seems to know that. In fact, half the world – I might exaggerate a little – knows that Dido Hoare now has the codex. Therefore, why is Ishmael Peters behaving as he does? You should tell me the answer when you've had a good night's rest. Sleep well.'

In the ninety seconds that it took me to fall into bed and pull up the duvet, the best explanation I'd managed was 'crazy as a jay bird', but even in my current semi-conscious state I knew that wouldn't satisfy me for longer than . . .

# Bedtime Story

The doorbell rang just as I was finishing the supper dishes. I wasn't expecting any visitors, so I made my way toward the sitting room, drying my hands on the kitchen towel and intending to take a careful look out the window before I answered the door.

Ben, who had been watching a cartoon on television, beat me to it. As I arrived, I found him standing on the settee, poking his head and shoulders out the open window.

He heard me coming, and wriggled back in, his eyes wide. He whispered, 'It's the Gruffalo!'

Intrigued, I took his place at the window, leaned out, and saw what he meant: a tubby, big-bellied man with a ponytail standing in the shadow of the little porch, rocking on his heels, rubbing his hands and waiting for me. Actually, he didn't seem to have the Gruffalo's horns and tusks. Good.

I said, 'You stay here. I'll go and let him in.' I took another quick look at the street without being able to find anything unusual there, checked that my keys were in my pocket, and shut and locked the door of the flat behind me as I went – just in case.

When I opened the downstairs door, he said, 'Hi,' and waited.

I said, 'You'd better come in,' and stood aside for him so that I could cast a final look out along the street. On the landing I said, 'I'm glad you stopped by, because I wanted to talk to you, but I'd better warn you that Ben is still up.'

He held up his hands. 'I'll be good.'

I said, 'Yes, you will,' and he threw me a funny look.

Ben was standing in the middle of the sitting room, and

I noticed he had turned the television off right in the middle of the cartoon.

Peters said, 'Hi, Ben. How are you?'

Ben said he was fine and went on staring, and when Peters accepted my instructions to sit, and placed himself in a corner of the settee, Ben went and sat down firmly beside him and went on staring. It might have bothered another man, but Peters just smiled at him and asked how old he was.

'I'm four. How old are you?'

'I'm a hundred years old.'

'You're not as old as my Grandpa!' Ben said indignantly.

'You can't be sure of that,' Peters told him. 'It's different with different people.'

I had sat down in the desk chair, facing them both so that I could watch his face while we talked.

'I wanted to get hold of you,' I said. 'Sorry to interrupt, but we don't have a lot of time. I need some information. What can you tell me about a company in Texas called Tylor Insurance? And a man who says he works for them – Richard Tipton?'

For a moment I thought he was having a heart attack, but he controlled himself with what looked like a heroic effort. 'You've seen them? They're here?'

'Tipton walked into the shop yesterday afternoon.'

'What did he say?'

'That he had been sent by his employer to buy the codex.'

'Oh,' Peters said. 'Wow. What . . . what did you tell him?'

'I told him that the codex is a fake. A modern forgery. I explained that I'd offered it for sale to somebody who is sending it back because he could tell it's a forgery.'

'Really? Then what did he say?'

'He said that he still wants to buy it, and he's coming back tomorrow to look at it.'

Peters's florid face went pale. 'Don't,' he said again. 'Don't do it, don't talk to him. I told you about this guy before, you know.'

'I thought he was probably the one you meant. But—'

'Look,' he said quickly. 'Maybe we shouldn't talk about this right now, on account of the kid. I guess he's going to go to bed soon, and he'd find it pretty boring. Ben, would you like me to tell you a bedtime story?'

'Would you read me a book?' Ben asked.

Peters nodded; Ben shot out of the room and rushed back with his copy of *The Gruffalo*, which he handed over and then waited to see whether Peters would recognize himself. Apparently he didn't. I waited until they had progressed to the third or fourth page of verse, and then muttered something about finishing the washing-up and crept out of the room, leaving the door wide open so that I could eavesdrop. When I heard a conversation starting up to mark the end of the reading, I returned. Ben had snuggled under Peters's arm in the interval, and the two of them were in a serious discussion about whether you would have to be really brave to play with the Gruffalo.

I said, 'Bedtime. No bath tonight, it's too late. You go and get ready and climb into bed, and I'll come and say good night.'

Ben climbed down slowly. He held out his hand, and Peters shook it.

'Will you come back?' Ben asked him.

Peters said, 'I'd like to do that, but I'm going away on a trip tomorrow. Maybe I can come when I get back to London. OK? Off you go, then. Good night.'

I said, 'He likes you. You're good with kids.'

'Am I? Who knows? I never had one of my own. It must be interesting, raising a little kid.'

'It makes you very careful,' I offered. 'Defensive.'

'Yeah.'

'So you have to expect me to be a little careful, with what's going on.'

He giggled. 'Well, me too. I've been being real careful ever since Tipton turned up in Amsterdam, believe me. Wish I'd started a bit earlier, but that's history. Wish I hadn't let Gabe "help" me. I wish all sorts of things. Spilled milk. It's killing me.'

I focussed on one thing he had said before. 'So you're running away again? Tomorrow? Because of Tipton?'

'I'd go tonight if I could get my things together that quick.'

196

'Where?'

'What do you mean?'

'Where can you go? Are you sure they won't just find you again?'

'This time, I'm going to drop so far out of sight that the Devil couldn't find me.'

'Right,' I said. 'And you'd advise me to do the same?'

He stared at me for a long moment. 'You can't.'

'That's right. I'm glad we understand each other. Since I can't, I am going to sell them the codex for as much cash as I can talk him into paying. Mr Peters, just what is the Tylor Insurance Company?'

'They sell car insurance and stuff in Texas. The owner is a rich old bastard.'

'And who is Richard Tipton?'

'He's worked for them for a long time. He's crazy, you know. What they call a psychopath. He doesn't have a conscience. You should know that.'

'Then all the more reason for me to give him what he wants and take away any reason he has to harm me, or Ben, or anybody else.'

'But I gave him what he wanted,' Peters said, 'and I'm not safe. He said to me he can get me any time he wants to.'

'Why would he want to?'

'Because I know something they want to wipe out, so as soon as they can they'll wipe *me* out.'

'Like Gabriel Steen.' That was the point when I heard Ben calling. 'I'm going to say good night. I'll just be a minute. Mr Peters, if I hear you move, I'll probably kill you myself before you reach the front door, because I am feeling pretty edgy.'

He said, 'Don't be silly,' in an offended tone, and I turned my back on him and went out, feeling fairly hopeful that he would still be there when I got back.

When I did, he said, 'I need a drink. You got anything?'

I reached into the cupboard, produced my father's Irish whiskey and a glass . . . followed on second thoughts by another glass, then poured two moderate shots and handed him one. I had a choice of questions for him. I didn't want any more details of what he had done the day Gabriel Steen had been killed, so we could skip that part.

'Why did they set the fire in your studio?'

'Because I kind of inherited some of Renaud's workshop.'

'And why are they so anxious to get their hands on Gabriel's fake manuscript?'

I wasn't expecting his laugh. 'Because it's a trap. For them. There's something in it that shows it's a fake, and exactly the same thing is in another manuscript that this guy in Texas already owns. It isn't easy to find, but it's there. It means that their manuscript isn't worth anything, either.'

'So if they bought mine they could destroy it and keep it from being traced to Renaud, and nor could theirs be?' Maybe it made sense. Provided that the 'clue' wasn't one of the things which had been passed on to people by Dr Fletcher – or Ernie. If it had, then they were already too late; but if it hadn't, then they would be in a hurry to make sure it didn't. Oh. All right.

'What is this trap?' I asked forcefully.

'A name.'

'What name? Yours?'

'Mine? Of course not, how could that happen? They bought their manuscript from a European dealer when I was still a teenager. No, it's just the name – Renaud.'

I could feel light dawning. 'The old forger. I know about him. He went to prison.'

I'd startled him again. I couldn't let it go just yet – I hate leaving stones unturned. 'Did he forge the Van Gogh, or did you?'

'How do you . . .?' He stopped for a moment to breathe. 'Does it matter? Renaud picked me up in Paris because I'm an artist. He taught me a lot. We worked together for a coupla years.'

'And he made the *Telschi*?'

'Yeah, long before I knew him. He sold it in New York for forty thousand dollars, and this guy who owns it now has it insured for four million.'

As a person would say, that's inflation for you.

'And who made the codex I have?'

'I . . . I told you – I inherited some of Renaud's old materials.'

I was trying to think it through. 'So they think that if they get the codex, they can destroy it and then it won't be proof that theirs is a fake?' They were already too late, if that was any satisfaction. People knew; and one of them had already identified it as a fraud. It was only a step for everyone to put two and two together. It might take longer to prove it, but I was getting the beginnings of an idea how that could be done. And I couldn't forget about Ernie and his discussion group, who had started an international exchange and spread the news everywhere, to everybody. Someone in the far mountains of the Hindu Kush had probably learned all about our great discovery two or three days ago.

'Do you mind if I . . .?'

I waved permission, and he emptied the bottle into his glass. Then we both sat for a while looking into our drinks and, in my case, trying to see what it all meant.

Peters could run away, or at least he would try to. I couldn't. All I could do is make the problem run away, which meant getting rid of Tipton. With about half a lifetime's portion of good luck, tomorrow would accomplish that. Was there anything I'd forgotten?

'You're leaving early in the morning?'

'Mmm.'

'I don't even want to know where. You can phone me if you like and find out whether my idea worked – whether they bought the manuscript, whether I got paid. Just don't do the silent phone call thing any more. It's boring. Speak. Leave a message on the machine. Tell me something useful, like when you'll try again.'

He was shaking his head. 'I don't wanna leave my voice on a machine anywhere. If the machine answers, then I hang up. It's safer. So far as they're concerned, there's too much that can go wrong and I won't risk it, right?'

Oh. So that was it? I shrugged.

He downed the rest of the whiskey like a glass of water and struggled to his feet. 'Better go.'

'Go safely,' I said coldly. 'Mind your step.'

'I'm all right.'

'Good!'

'Take care of the kid.'

'I do,' I said.

When I opened the street door, I noticed that he wasn't too drunk to move very carefully. From the shadows, he looked up and down the street. Then he said, 'Don't worry about me,' and left.

I locked the door and put up the chain before I dragged myself upstairs. It was still early, and I was still stressed out. I went to bed.

# Trap

I got back to the shop a little after nine, carelessly swinging a supermarket carrier bag which had held our catalogue printout when I left, and now contained Gabriel's codex. It actually felt safer that way than if I tried to hide it under my coat. I unlocked the door, re-locked it, turned off the security alarm, and disappeared into the office, shutting the door behind me. Then I pulled the manuscript out of the bag, unwrapped it, set it down beside the computer, and couldn't keep myself from opening it just to look at a couple of the folios and wonder how much of somebody's lifetime the whole fake would represent.

The phone rang twice and then cut out: that was a signal. When the second call came, I listened for Laura Smiley's voice and then greeted her.

'You're back. You've got it?'

'It's all right.'

'Then I'll come over. I have some news, and I need to get some information from you.'

I told her that I wouldn't go away.

When I heard the rattling at the door, I went out to answer it and found myself staring through the glass at the person who had just arrived – a stranger, a faded middle-aged woman wearing a grey cloth coat which hung unbuttoned over what looked like a cotton coverall. She held a shopping bag in one hand, and an old plastic handbag in the other.

I opened the door a little nervously.

'Hallo,' the woman said in a heavy Eastern European accent. 'I am Anna. I come to clean for you. You are Dido Hoare.'

Anna? Oh. It was very good. I stood aside, invited her in, and locked up again.

201

'I am thorsty,' the woman commented. 'You haff coffee?'
'I'll start it,' I said. 'I could use some myself. What country
do you come from?'

'Does it matter?' Sergeant Smiley said in her own voice.
'Let's say Lithuania. And we ought to get out of sight before
you spoil everything by laughing like that. Besides, I have
something to tell you.'

We sat beside the desk while our coffee was brewing and
looked at each other solemnly.

'First of all, I got hold of Alan Quinn this morning, and
he contacted Hertz in Harwich. They sent him the details
of the driver's license of the man who hired the car
the morning that Gabriel Steen was killed. They're wrong:
the license number belongs to somebody with another name
who lives at a different address. So he's got Hertz to report
the car as stolen. That gives us some leeway in how we
handle it if your friends turn up. Secondly, they've been
gathering fingerprints and DNA from the hire car that was
burned out. There's quite a lot of material, and some of it
might turn out to be relevant. He's going to drive in this
morning, and Essex will be collaborating officially with
anything we do.'

'They might just phone me, you know.'

'I don't think so,' she said. 'If they do, fine, no harm done.
But I imagine they'll come in person. That's what I'm here
to think about. What's out there?' She indicated the door in
the back wall.

I got up, slid back the bolts, unlocked the lock, and threw
the door open on to my little paved back garden with its
decor of weather-beaten wooden shed, climbing frame with
swing, two dead plants in flower pots, and a disused dustbin.
She went out, I followed her. The area was surrounded by
twelve-foot-high brick walls.

'What's the easiest way of getting in and out of here?'

'You could stand on the dustbin and climb into the garden
next door over the roof of the shed,' I suggested. It was one
of Mr Spock's regular routes. 'Or you could probably climb
out the other side.' There was a corner on the southern side
where it was possible to scramble up some projecting bricks

and clamber on to the top of the wall, where you would find yourself standing ten feet above the tiny space beside the house which held the wheelie bin. She made notes. We went back inside and pulled the door shut again.

'Don't lock it,' she said sharply. 'Shut it but leave it unlocked. Wait a minute, we'll push the bolts a little way across so that it's harder to see that they haven't been pushed home. We want to have a back exit available.'

'Or entrance?' I suggested – but I couldn't see the elegant Mr Tipton choosing to scramble over the shed roof in broad daylight. I said, 'What's going to happen?'

'If we're lucky, nothing. We'll just have to play it by ear. Look, you did say that you wanted to do this.'

I said, 'I have to finish it.'

'Then try not to worry.'

There was no point trying to get any work done. When I heard the post arrive I went out to get it, but I wasn't interested enough to look at the envelopes. I threw them on to the packing table for later. Anna-Laura wrapped a cotton scarf around her hair, filled the bucket and took that and the mop out into the shop where she would make a show of using them if anybody turned up to notice anything. Basically we were both waiting for two o'clock.

We spent much of the time drinking coffee and watching the cars in the road: neighbours' cars, strangers' cars, delivery vans. But she had been right: it was just after twelve thirty when the car we were watching out for slid past the display window and parked in front of the door. I was hiding behind the office door before there was time for it to disgorge the two men.

My cleaner muttered, 'Knew it.' She inserted what looked like a big hearing aid into her left ear. There was a rattling at the door. She was just starting to say, 'All right?' Oddly enough, she wasn't talking to me, although she was again when she said, 'You'd better pretend I'm not here.' I pushed myself forward to unlock the door.

Tipton came inside with his briefcase in his hand and his eyes on Anna. She had just spilled water in the far aisle, and was swilling at it with the mop.

203

I said, 'I wasn't expecting to hear from you for a couple of hours. Never mind, it's all right.' I followed the direction of his gaze, and called, 'Anna?'

She stopped what she was doing and waited.

'Anna, you go on with your work.'

'Sorry, I no . . . I no hear you say.' She cupped her hand behind her left ear, pretending to be a bit deaf.

I made an effort, speaking very slowly and clearly. 'You clean here. I will finish business soon. Soon.'

'I finish soon,' she said stolidly.

'We'll go into the office,' I said to Tipton. 'It's in there.'

He followed me in. I handed him the little book. He looked at the vellum binding without the slightest change of expression, then opened the cover and looked at a couple of the folios.

'I do think it's a forgery,' I told him to fill the silence.

He nodded. 'Where did you get it?'

'A book scout brought it in. He said he got it in Italy. But I don't know anything about that. I'll sell it to you, if you really want it. I'll sell it "as is", without any guarantees of any kind. You're just buying what you have in your hands, that's all.'

'How much?'

'Twenty thousand,' I said.

'Twenty thousand dollars.'

A noise of machinery out in the street was growing louder. I closed the office door quickly to shut out that distraction.

'And you'll throw in the digital photos you've taken of it. I know about those.'

I hesitated, but I didn't try to hide the little greedy smirk that was starting to stretch my mouth. 'All right. If you've brought the cash, I'll write you a receipt for it.'

I went over and pulled the envelope out of the top drawer, spilling the prints in a heap on the desk. He stirred through them and pretended to be looking at a few, but he couldn't really be bothered. He must have known that the digital images would be on the camera's memory card, and in the computer too if I'd printed these out myself, but he was pretending not to understand the way that these things worked, and so was I, even if it made no sense.

He put the codex and the pictures down together on the desk, opened his briefcase, pulled out a bulky manila envelope, dropped it on the desk, and slid everything he was buying into his case. If I started to look uneasy, that wasn't an act. I shivered.

The noise out in the street was getting louder, a kind of rusty squeal of stressed machinery.

'All right,' I said suddenly, giving the benefit of the doubt to the contents of the envelope because time was running out fast. I opened the long drawer of the desk, found our receipts book in which I scrawled the words 'For one anon. Codex, 178 folios, as is, $20,000', carefully added the date and my signature, and handed him the top copy of that to go with the slippery pile of the manuscript and photos.

He was just snapping that shut when there was a kind of hollow metallic bang from outside. He noticed it this time, raised his head, grabbed the briefcase, yanked the office door open and looked down the aisle toward the window. The shape of his car was there beyond the glass, dangling and swinging from the hydraulic arm of a transporter lorry. A traffic warden appeared to be supervizing its removal. On the other hand, a policeman whom I did not recognize, with a plain-clothes officer who was Alan Quinn, were standing very close to Mr Tipton's driver. They seemed to be saying something to him, but I couldn't see him talking back.

Tipton took a running step towards the front of the shop, reaching with his right hand under his open coat.

Suddenly my cleaning lady was there, her gaze focussed on the hidden hand. 'Don't be so stupid,' she snapped. Then she swung the mophead hard against his eyes. Blinded by dirty water, he staggered backwards. I gave him a hard push in the small of his back, she stuck a leg behind one of his and pulled on the arm that was now rising in the air, and he went down on his face. She had one foot on his shoulder and dragged his right arm straight back and upwards. The hand was empty, which seemed to demonstrate that Tipton was also a quick thinker. At that same moment, there came a gust of fresh air at my back, and two uniformed policemen wearing body armour appeared through the suddenly open door. They must have climbed over the wall.

That was the moment when Smiley explained, 'Richard Tipton, I am arresting you on suspicion of conspiracy to commit a murder.' There was the formulaic warning to be added to that, but nobody was really listening. From the blank look on his face, even the suspect was lost in his own thoughts.

Then a lot more people came in and things became noisy and busy. I sat down in the desk chair and leaned back, wondering why I felt so calm and relaxed now, and let them get on with it. Everything was a little unreal. But comfortable. When I remembered, I picked up the phone and rang Barnabas. When he answered I said, 'It's all right if you want to come over now. It's finished.'

# Afterwards

Ben had gone to bed, and Barnabas had left – mostly because he thought I ought to go to bed too. It had been a hard day. The orders from the catalogue had begun to taper off, but they were still coming in at a fair pace, and a lot of the day had been spent by Ernie and me in billing, wrapping, and walking to and from the post office. The rest of it had been packing boxes. The London Book Fair was on at the weekend, and I was starting to get ready for it.

Bath. Definitely.

The moment that I realized how terribly necessary it was to go and lie down in hot water, with bubbles, for at least half an hour, the doorbell rang.

I closed my eyes.

When it rang again, I struggled upright, wobbled over to the window, and hauled it up.

I might have known. I *would* have known, except that I'd assumed he was somewhere far away: Ishmael Peters standing out in the middle of the pavement looking up at the windows.

He waved and said, 'Hi.'

I didn't wave back but said, 'Wait a minute. Then I went down to let him in.

When we got into the sitting room he started by looking around, then sat with a thump on the settee and asked, 'Ben asleep?'

I said firmly, 'Yes, and so am I. You're back?'

'On my way to Amsterdam. I phoned the lawyers, and they told me about the arrests. Your police got the evidence to prosecute? So I can go back to Gabe's flat now. For a while, anyway. I don't know how long. Hey, I don't know that I want to stay there any more. But it'll give me time to think.'

His voice faded. I nodded vaguely.

'I'm going to let it out. Let out about the Telschi, I mean. From my manuscript. It's going to come out that it's a forgery anyway. So I had to thank you, before I go.'

'Why?'

'Well, the way I heard, you stopped it. Stopped them.'

He said it as though it had been something like a twenty-first-century version of the gunfight at the O.K. Corral – beautiful woman defeats outlaw gang single-handed with her dainty Derringer.

'That's true,' I said.

'People are going to figure it all out anyway, from my manuscript. Tipton was too late, wasn't he? Your photos did it. But I might as well save everybody the work.'

I thought, '*my* manuscript.' And then I thought about Barnabas happily e-mailing back and forth with the researcher in Oslo, and the messages on the discussion group. Over three thousand, last time I looked.

He was getting to his feet. 'I'm sorry I came too late to say good night to Ben. He's a nice little kid. Tell him good-bye from the Gruffalo.'

I said, 'I don't think you need to bother about publicizing the forgery. I think people enjoy working that out themselves. Anyway, I've sold it.'

'You sold . . .'

'The codex.'

He was speechless for a long, long time. Then he managed, 'What? How did you do that?'

I said very gently, 'We sent pictures of parts of the manuscript to an internet discussion group. And somebody in Oslo contacted a man about it, and he contacted us. An American. He owns about half of the internet, and he's a big Telschi enthusiast. He saw our pictures, and he said what a *good* forgery it is, and told us he wanted to buy it as a "modern replica".'

Peters was stunned, but managed to ask, 'How much did you sting him for?'

'Twenty thousand dollars.'

His face crumpled up and he started to laugh.

I went over to the desk, opened a drawer in the top, and pulled out something that I'd been keeping there for when he finally did turn up.

'I've kept two thousand pounds to cover my expenses. I've given Ernie a thousand pounds for all his help. It'll get him through his final exams this spring. There's just over fifteen thousand dollars left.'

I walked over and dropped the roll of hundred dollar bills into his lap. Then I went and opened the door and waited. After a moment he followed me, hesitated, then kept on going down the stairs. I started down after him, and he opened the door at the bottom, stopped again, and turned around. He was probably going to say something stupid.

'Mr Peters,' I said, and stopped long enough to censor my words. 'Mr Peters, just go away.'

He said, 'Call me Ishmael.'

I could hear the annoying falsetto giggle all the way down the road.

# Afterword

## The Real Telschi Manuscript

When the great art forger Marcel Renaud created the Telschi Manuscript, his genius was to create a hoax of something so unprecedented that it would be almost impossible for anyone to ever prove it a hoax. Except, of course, Renaud's one-time student, Ishmael Peters. The Telschi was made by Renaud long before Peters came on to the scene. But when Peters read a magazine article about the Telschi describing a theory of how the mystery language was created using a variant of the Cardan grille method, that was enough to make alarm bells ring in the mind of the old forger's one-time protégé. Peters is no code-breaker and could not do what so many Telschi enthusiasts had failed to do and crack the cipher, but he did have one advantage – he possessed much of the contents of Renaud's old workshop, including a series of his old grilles, sheets of cardboard with window holes cut into them. One of these grilles was a key to a very simple steganographic code – laid over the last page of the manuscript it reveals six characters that can, with a little imagination, be read as plain Latin characters: R-E-N-A-U-D. When his friend Gabriel Steen returned from Italy with a bundle of five-century-old vellum, Peters was able to create a good visual likeness of his former master's greatest hoax. However, it was an imperfect copy, and those imperfections are what showed up in the analysis that Fletcher, Barnabas and his Oslo colleague performed.

Although the Telschi Manuscript has no precedent in Dido's world, it does in ours. Barnabas can think himself fortunate that while Dido was trying to crack the mystery of Steen's murder, he had only an imitation of the Telschi mystery to crack.

The real-world inspiration for Telschi is a strange 240-page document in the Beinecke Rare Book Library at Yale University, catalogue number MS408, popularly known as the Voynich Manuscript. This extraordinary document, sometimes dubbed 'the most mysterious manuscript in the world', is written in a text that has defied any definitive interpretation by the world's linguists and code-breakers since it was brought to light in 1912, and is heavily illustrated in an almost equally mysterious manner. For example, of the many plants illustrated throughout the pages, only two or three have been identified with any degree of certainty. And unlike Renaud's Telschi Manuscript in Dido's world, the Voynich Manuscript is almost certainly the real thing. In 1912, the Jesuit Collegio Romano sold part of a collection of manuscripts kept at the villa Mondragone in Frascati to a Polish–American antiquarian book dealer, Wilfrid Voynich. The manuscript that now bears his name was by far the strangest item in that collection. Although there were some at the time who suspected Voynich himself was behind the manuscript, it has been possible to trace some of the work's history.

We know that in the early 17th century it was owned by one Georg Baresch, a little-known alchemist of Prague. Convinced that he had in his possession the key to a great mystery, Baresch contacted Athanasius Kircher, a Jesuit scholar famed for his work on Coptic, suggesting to Kircher that he was the one person best suited to understand the mysteries of this 'sphinx' of a manuscript. One of Baresch's letters to Kircher has recently been uncovered and is the earliest reference we have to the manuscript.

After Baresch's death, the manuscript was passed on to Johannes Marcus Marci, of Charles University, Prague, who continued the correspondence with Kircher and finally sent the manuscript to him. According to Marci's letter, which is now attached to the manuscript, his own research led him to believe that the manuscript had once been bought by

211

Emperor Rudolf II of Bohemia (1552–1612), who believed it to be the work of the English friar, scientist and code-smith, Roger Bacon. If so, the seller was the mysterious and shady John Dee, a kind of Elizabethan cross between James Bond and Gandalf, whom Barnabas mentions in Chapter 39. Dee had an interest in Bacon and owned some of his manuscripts. This is the conclusion that Wilfrid Voynich himself favoured, although the manuscript does not appear to be early enough or in the right style for Bacon.

What then? There is a good chance that the Voynich is, indeed, a forgery: not a modern one by any means, but a creation of Dee or his shadowy colleague Edward Kelley. They spent some time in Bohemia trying to persuade the Emperor of the value of their services, and have something of a dodgy reputation – Enochian script, the 'Angelic language' that Kelley dictated at length to Dee, bears some faint similarities to 'Voynichese'. It is true that there is no known mention of the Voynich manuscript in Dee's records, but then if the pair of them were trying to con the Emperor out of six hundred ducats it's possible he would have been no more keen to have anything in writing than Peters is to have his voice recorded on answering machines.

Since the rediscovery of the manuscript in 1912, it has become a phenomenon. Put Voynich into an internet search engine and you'll get around a third of a million hits. Dozens of theories have been put forwards to explain it, from the elaborately mathematical to the outright lunatic. The problem is that it just defies simple understanding. It has certain characteristics in common with natural languages, such as following some form of orthographic rule, and a rough correspondence with Zipf's law of word frequency. As would be expected, there are words that appear to have context, so that for example in the section that apparently deals with astronomy there are words that might indicate 'star' or 'constellation' and do not appear elsewhere. On the other hand there are words that are repeated three times in a row, and there is a strange bell-curve distribution of word length – that is to say that there is a great tendency for words to be of similar lengths and, unlike any European languages, there are few short or very long words. This has led some to suggest that it might be an early attempt to write an oriental language such as Vietnamese or Manchu in an artificial European style script, but most people would argue that it is either an artificial language, such as Dee and Kelley's Enochian, or an elaborate and as yet undeciphered code.

In 2003 Gordon Rugg, a researcher at the University of Keele, announced that he had, if not actually cracked the code, found the most likely way it was created. Rugg's hypothesis is that the Voynich was a hoax perpetrated by Kelley, who undoubtedly had a great interest in codes and was familiar with the Cardan Grille process. Rugg showed that, using a table of characters and a number of grilles, one can recreate a very reasonable visual match to the Voynich text by placing the grilles over a random character and creating the rest of a word by taking the characters shown in the following windows of the grille. He has yet to produce a text by this method that matches the word length distributions and entropic values of original Voynichese; and until he can, his theory will remain just one of many, if a rather compelling one. It is, of course, this method that Renaud used to create the somewhat simpler text of the Telschi manuscript that so troubles Dido and Barnabas in this novel.

There may be a secret message hidden in the Voynich text. It certainly appears alchemical, and perhaps the mysterious nature of the pictures suggests that the entire thing is an elaborate esoteric code that we will simply never understand without some lost key. Perhaps the code will be cracked one day, or perhaps the real message is a steganographic code, hidden like Renaud's signature in the Telschi, where it will likely never be discovered. Or maybe there is nothing in it at all, and it is merely an elaborate glossolalia created by a madman. Or perhaps simplest of all it is intentionally complex yet devoid of all meaning, an elaborate hoax intended to gull the gullible, and that Kelley was – like Renaud – simply after some money. If so, then like the fellow who owns half the internet and buys the pseudo-Telschi at the end of this book, let's remember that it's enough to enjoy it for what it is. Peters had not sold a work of art for that much money for some years; he should be pleased with himself.

Further reading on the web:

http://www.voynich.nu
The Voynich Manuscript (tons of information, including complete scans)

http://mcs.open.ac.uk/gr768/about/index.shtml
Gordon Rugg's home page

http://www.voynich.net
The home of the Voynich Manuscript Mailing list

http://webtext.library.yale.edu/beinflat/pre1600.ms 408.htm
Catalogue description of the Voynich at Yale, including links to a complete scan of the manuscript